# AMARANTH-SAGE EPIPHANIES
## OF
## DUSK-WEAVING PARADISE

# AMARANTH-SAGE EPIPHANIES OF DUSK-WEAVING PARADISE

Selected poems of

## Hugo G. Walter

FITHIAN PRESS ❦ SANTA BARBARA, CALIFORNIA ❦ 1995

PUBLISHED BY FITHIAN PRESS
A DIVISION OF DANIEL AND DANIEL, PUBLISHERS, INC.
POST OFFICE BOX 1525
SANTA BARBARA, CALIFORNIA 93102


LIBRARY OF CONGRESS CATALOGING-IN-PUBLICATION DATA
    Walter, Hugo
        Amaranth-sage epiphanies of dusk-weaving paradise : Selected poems of
    Hugo Walter / Hugo Walter.
            p.   cm.
        ISBN 1-56474-109-5
        I. Title.
    PS3573.A472283A6   1994
    811'.54—dc20                                    94-18969
                                                    CIP

# Contents

## The Soul of the Universe

Preserving the Heart of the Universe / 13
A Delphic-Winding Castle / 14
I Am a Gobelin-Emerald Reverie / 15
The Soul of the Twilight Sea / 16
A Grail of Autumn-Sceptered Light / 17
The Soul of the Mantlepiece / 18
The Spirit of the Palladian Bridge / 19
Of Tarantella-Apsed Clouds / 20
The Soul of the Dance I / 21
I Am the Spirit of the Sunlight / 22
In Moss-Helixed Synergies / 23
Across the Sea of Galilee / 24
I Opened a Star / 25
Shaping the Figures of the Dance / 26
A Salmon-Shadowed Figure / 27
Pilasters of Soft-Dewed Omnipotence / 28
Across Arcadian Meadows / 29
The Soul of the Dance II / 30
A Dance of Twelve Souls / 31
Odyssey-Pale Tears / 33
A Cerulean-Ancient Cerebrum / 34
A Flower on the Coffin / 35
Amaranth-Emulating Tremors of Eternity / 36
Shaping the Gothic-Liminal Heart / 37
When Twilight Falls / 38
A Face of Ancient-Palomar Dreams / 39
What if God / 40
A Syrinx-Trembling Ring / 42
The Isenheim Altarpiece / 43
The Evening Clouds / 44
An Orange-Dryadic Sun / 45
Eroica-Modulating Epiphanies / 46
The Angels of the Annunciation / 47

Saving the Dreams of Hermes / 48
Of Amstel-Vaned Solitudes / 49
The Poem / 50
A Mist of Marigold-Intuitive Communions / 51
A Millennial-Sacred Grove / 52
I Am a Goldau-Misting Tapestry / 53
Self-Transformation / 54
I Am the Rubens-Panelled Soul / 55
The Soul of the Universe / 56
I Am the Soul of the Twilight / 58
The Apollonian-Sage Bridge / 59
I Am an Amber-Prophetic Stone / 60

THE LIGHT OF THE DANCE

The Light of the Dance / 63
Of Phoenix-Dewed Constellations / 64
The Threshold-Wind / 65
A New Jersey Sunset / 66
The Anemone-Green Eyes of Evening / 67
The Home of the Butterflies / 68
Two Monarchs / 70
Twilight Invocations of Dusk-Mourning Beauty / 71
Let the Soul of Nature Be Your Soul / 72
A Maya-Purple Flower / 74
The Divinations of the Wind / 75
Mother Nature / 76
The Pool of Water Lilies / 77
The Wind Is a Dionysian Sharing / 78
In Swan-Gloaming Blossoms / 79
The Soul of the Forest / 80
The Voices of the Clouds / 81
An Infinity of Sensibility / 82
In the Tempest-Driven Heart / 83
The Kinetic-Autumn Wind / 84
Gazelle-White Cylinders / 85
The Snow-Shower / 86
The Mist People / 87

A Hidden Lake / 88
Nothing but Sea and Sky / 89
The Flower of Eternity / 90
The Morning Dew Is a Dance of Divine Whispers / 91
Of Auburn-Etching Lazarus / 92
A Clock Rides Upon the Sea / 93
The First Sounds of Spring / 94
Of Glynde-Spacious Eternity / 95
A Madonna / 96
A Damask-Scrolled Fugue / 97
In Mimosa-Yellow Incantations / 98
The Sunset Clouds / 99
Of Sacred-Anemone Silences / 100
Autumn / 101
Along the Avalon-Misting Shore / 102
Bronze-Parabled Leaves / 103
The Purification / 104
The Voice of Eternity / 105
Let the Autumn Fill Your Soul / 106
Of Heliotrope-Mimosa Dawn / 107
An Amethyst-Glistening Petal / 108
The Soul of the Lake / 109
The Twilight-Apocalyptic Reverie / 110

## Of Divine-Gloaming Wisdom and Eden-Exalting Spaces

The Wings of Swans / 113
The Source of Immortal Time / 114
Echoes of Eternity / 115
A Sculpture of Orange-Chasmed Leaves / 116
Threshold Moments / 117
Four Sacred Forms / 118
A Dahlia-Globed Oasis / 119
Of Dusk-Gloaming Mirrors / 120
An Ethereal-Sage Castle / 121
Of Divine-Gloaming Wisdom / 122
A Timeless Moment / 123
A Stone-Breathing Manor House / 124

Through Marble-Misting Eons / 125
The Figures in the Paintings / 126
Of Atlantis-Shaping Souls / 127
The Pristine Tapestry / 128
Shaping Ancient Cosmogonies / 129
Of Ivory-Tympanum Silences / 130
As Emerald-Amorphous Breezes Vanish / 131
Of Magenta-Vernal Hieroglyphs / 132
Through the Heart of Time / 133
Coral-Adagio Helixes / 134
In the Briny-Spectral Deep / 135
Of Rosary-Incarnate Light / 136
An Orphic Heart / 137
Of the Poppy-Breathing Chandelier / 138
Salisbury-Myrrh Incandescences / 139
The Virgin of the Rocks / 140
A Silent-Solstice Figure / 141
Of Elysian-Prophetic Eternity / 142
Through the Moon Gate / 143
A Village Beyond Time / 144
In An Elysian-Petaled Cove / 145
The Spirit of the Manse / 146
A Chandelier of Maroon-Contemplating Light / 147
In the Great Chamber / 148
The Ghost at Kenilworth / 149
A Castle of White-Hummingbird Silences / 150
In Emerald-Veiled Panoplies / 151
An Orpheus-Reigning Oasis / 152
The First Cycle of Mortality / 153
In a Timeless Vale / 154
A Sacred-Liminal Well / 155
The Caretaker of Time's Garden / 156
A Castle by the Sea / 157

Afterword by J.M. Daniel / 158

# Amaranth-Sage Epiphanies
## of
# Dusk-Weaving Paradise

# THE SOUL OF THE UNIVERSE

# PRESERVING THE HEART OF THE UNIVERSE

I walk through the ancient-calypso cemetery
In Kandinsky-almandine reflections of twilight-
Consecrating silences listening to the voices
Of lichen-engraving stones speaking of dusk-
Orange blooms of gladiolus-soaring light
Listening to the voices of tempest-lacquered
Tantra-chalices speaking of the divinely pure-
White heart of Apollonian-profound cloud-dreams
Listening to the voices of the evening sea
Shaping the emerald-generating apertures
Of a Cyclades-traversing temple along the deluge-
    sceptered, tiara-misting shore

I walk through the clouds in apocalyptic homage
To Sistine-galactic solitudes whispering yellow-
Tonal auras of timelessness to passing meteors
Of purple-angular light shaping frescoes
Of hibiscus-concentric reveries on synthetic-
Webbed, Munch-tentacled aspirations
Of crystalline-moist moon-dances
Preserving the heart of the universe
In the saffron-gloaming streams, symphonic-
Lavender aureoles, and chrysalis-mazed, cypress-
Diastolic harmonic-visions of my light-conceiving,
    sunset-redeeming soul.

# A DELPHIC-WINDING CASTLE

I am the fertile-cairned, Redon-chrysalis silence
At the dahlia-globed heart of the orange-cypress-pinioned,
Pomegranate-confessing tree

A Corot-white castle of cyclamen-perpetual autumns
Shears the crimson-leavened twilight from convolvulus-
Requiemed skies into the mimosa-cavernous apparitions
Of its own Cecilia-enshrining heart

Crystalline-turquoise butterflies and Hesperus-rising masks
Of pearl-helixed wisdom seal chrysanthemum-ringed souls
In jade-melodic, Cybele-deepening meoises
Of Neuschwanstein-adamanthine light

A Delphic-winding castle of red-gloaming dreams
Vanishes in the auburn-effulgent silence of its own
Perpetuity unseen by mortal eyes except when the amaranth-
Templed wind rustles golden-webbed whispers of ancient-
Hermetic horizons across Nolde-sacred vases of zinnia-
Diapason exultations

I am the Böcklin-wise, unicorn-serenading silence
Shaping heron-magenta, diva-pilastered estuary-essences
In Turner-prophetic diffusions of marble-chambered,
Mellifluous-yellow light.

# I Am a Gobelin-Emerald Reverie

I am the saffron-lyred heart of the Nymphenburg-lavender
Stone shaping obelisk-singing, azalea-sweeping expanses
In celestial inclinations of Apollonian groves
Carving magnolia-enlightening, ivory-exalting truths
On grail-altared, forsythia-tinted auras of Tuscan-
Illimitable urns reshaping the garland-extending vista
Of merlin-shadowed, trefoil-cresting dreams in anemone-
Weaving, silver-misting Lucerne-silences
I am the Atlantis-liminal breath of the chandelier-
Germinating epiphany investing my soul in every other
Stone, the Beningbrough-permeating, jonquil-luminous spirit
Of the Arundel-perfecting isle of Cythere-embalming
Preludes, I am a Gobelin-emerald reverie of sublime-arching,
Cypress-templed timelessness redeeming mortality
In Ispahan-veined, magenta-rising transformations
Of twilight-saving, amber-gloaming stones infusing
Versailles-fragile, titan-amorphous pallors
With Meissen-crystalline, diamond-astered effusions
Of maroon-symphonic, Turner-effulgent light.

# THE SOUL OF THE TWILIGHT SEA

I am the soul of the asphodel-burgeoning universe
Permeating silver-lyred, jonquil-diffusing silences
Of Psyche-altared, nirvana-glistening light in amaranth-
Rising incarnations of moist-acanthus, Eleusinian-flowing,
Aegean-seminal dreams
I am the dusk-arching heart of the garden
Shaping chrysalis-lavender, Stygian-throned heavens
In Florentine-misting symmetries of medusa-plumed,
Empyrean-rippling moonlight
I am the spirit of divine light
Reclaiming the lily-gloaming heart of Blenheim-effulgent
Autumn from Ozymandias-cairned torrential-hours
Whispering poppy-meandering seeds of marble-pulsing,
Olana-germinating evening in Lethe-coursing absolutions
Of willow-emerald, fugal-pristine paradise
I am the soul of the twilight sea
Bearing marigold-prophetic chalices of calyx-floating
Stars and coral-enchanted smiles to the pearl-azure shore
Of sage-listening eternity shaping pyramid-scrolled cloud-
Haloes in grail-leavening tremors of Aeolian-saffron suns.

# A GRAIL OF AUTUMN-SCEPTERED LIGHT

I am a vase of salmon-crescent, Adonis-effulgent light
Rising from the ocean in an auburn-chorused reverie
Of asphodel-awakening, Rodin-elegiac annunciations

I am a grail of autumn-sceptered light ascending
Vetheuil-animating marrows of sky where only tessera-
Pale albatrosses and pink-gelatinous pulsations conceive
Pristine-jade folds of amulet-trembling calyx-winds

I am a chalice of mimosa-silver, amaryllis-passionate
Light transforming hourglass rituals
To divine-murmuring, Elysian-tender silences
Transmuting ancient-tidal veils of nightingale-cradled
Truth to perennial-white, Eden-dewed stars

I am a constellation of pearl-engraving rains,
Shiva-melodious chasms, and muse-generating ballet-
    tempiettos
Dissolving the maenad-viscous flux of agaric-lithesome,
Arctic-manacled rivulets in the amber-ethereal,
Willow-intense depth of sunset-perfecting,
Cathedral-shaping prophesies of Promethean-misting,
Emerald-resonating light.

# The Soul of the Mantlepiece

The Mansard-blue soul of the pomegranate-flourishing
Mantlepiece rises in marble-blossoming visions
Of diamond-lintelled solitude spreading ethereal-domed
Wisdom around the spacious-twilight chamber beyond
Triadic-virginal veils of ephemeral-mitred dust
The grail-sceptered soul of the Neuschwanstein-timeless
Mantlepiece filling the andante-tapestried room
With the sunflower-lambent perfection of its inner
Illumination floating pyramid-extending shadows
Of immutable delight across my horizon-conceiving,
Rembrandt-liminal mind shaping the amaranth-sacred
Beauty of sapphire-redeeming rainbows and autumn-
Helixed silences in Eroica-unvanquished, heliotrope-
Gleaming synergies of Pythian-omnipotent innocence
And emerald-lyred, Michelangelo-gloaming omniscience.

# THE SPIRIT OF THE PALLADIAN BRIDGE

I am the spirit of the Palladian bridge
Shaping Ionic-white, cedar-fluent passions
Of amaranth-sublime, acacia-cresting light
Across obelisk-blue pallors of Dardanelles-
Rusting, hydrangea-sated memories

I am the spirit of the snow-meandering silence
Knowing that all will come to pass that is in the heart
In golden-veiled paroxysms as the Scarisbrick-frail wind
Breathes amber-gloaming eaves of damask-prismed light
Across the green-listening, sapphire-inundating sea

I am the spirit of the Hyperion-consecrating court
Spreading the Handel-wise magnanimity of my soul
Into the jonquil-fermenting sky and the diamond-
Fusing horizon I am the harbinger of coniferous-
Eclectic dreams and sunset-secluding soliloquies

I am the diadem-apocalyptic blossom of lily-expanding
Life perpetuating helicon-lambent moor-silences
In wisteria-endless arabesques of saffron-concentric
Cloud-gladioli I am the Wilton-sealing destiny
Of threshold stones wandering in diastolic-orange,
Poppy-engraving mazes of twilight-pergola,
Orphic-soaring reveries.

## OF TARANTELLA-APSED CLOUDS

The Halifax-polygonal streaming of tarantella-apsed clouds
Drips fragile-mazed trees of purple-luminescent,
Crepuscular-sage blooms and magenta-pellucid megaliths
Of orchid-golding light onto marble-silent, sphinx-
Panelled fields as a Castalian-lonely figure shapes
The evening-tremulous, Olana-dewed wind in jade-leavening,
Mandarin-enthroning hieroglyphs of honey-myrtle,
Pink-almandine light carving his astral-tendrilled,
Onyx-gloaming soul on dusk-timeless, Elysian-pulsing
Whispers of the calyx-chastening, pearl-discoursing sea
And on Poseidon-templed truths of porcelain-epiphanic,
Minerva-pristine twilight.

## THE SOUL OF THE DANCE I

I am the Nataraja-perpetual soul of the dance
Carving staccato-laminating embers of jasmine-
Subliminal rhythms on miranda-embracing melodies
Of Parthenon-white, damask-pure light

I am the muse-astered soul of the dance
Pulsing porcelain-vaned tremors of the dusk-
Lyred divinity across auburn-leavening
Convergences of diamond-lintelled, astral-germinating
   epiphanies

I am the Fauve-tendrilled soul
Of the dance saving the twilight ballet
Of the sea from sable-sirocco, Lethe-wreathed
Dreams of Dorian-graceful partheneia floating
Albemarle-ethereal radiances of amber-philomel
Snow-arabesques in the apocalyptic-pale
Freedom of temple-destined, alcaic-turning light

I am the Nataraja-vaulting soul
Of the dance perpetuating Giverny-streaming,
Wisteria-glistening rituals of pomegranate-meadowed,
Sphinx-confessing eternity in mandala-soaring hearts
Of jonquil-diffusing, Aphrodite-helixed renascence.

# I AM THE SPIRIT OF THE SUNLIGHT

I am the spirit of the hyacinth-singing sunlight
As it weaves Beauvais-sonorous fusions
Of golden-mullioned silences and jade-
Glistening horizons in heliotrope-unfinished
Distances of crimson-duned, pantheon-
Iridescent solitudes I am a Stourhead-conceiving
Reverie of jonquil-diffusing light fulfilling
The shape of the sea in the Aeolian-prophetic
Destiny of my amber-architraved, iris-evolving
Soul I am an amethyst-sacred temple of auburn-
Cascading light carving Endymion-pale inflections
Of astral-wayward immortality on Salisbury-lichened
Agoras of chrysalis-corniced squalls in magenta-
Inventing, lilac-symphonic gardens.

# IN MOSS-HELIXED SYNERGIES

I am the Dionysian-martyred soul of the convolvulus-shoaled
Mausoleum shaping primordial-auburn blooms of allegretto-
Paned light in Rothamsted-pulsing expanses of crystalline-
Mazed solitudes

I hear the orange-diapason voices of Bernini-sceptered
Endlessness a thousand miles beyond the edge of time
And yet within the inner resonances, forever permeating
The crimson-stamened, Memnon-garlanding echoes
Of my diastolic-veined, magenta-nomadic soul

I am the marble-gentian spirit of Ascott-conjuring
Amplitudes of sapphic-holy, renaissance-conceiving light
Dissolving time in moss-helixed, cyclamen-vaulting synergies
Of Michelangelo-gloaming, rainbow-intense stones

I see the Aphrodite-lambent eyes of immortal-stained time
In sapphire-haloed tears of Promethean-lyred pallors
I feel the nocturne-splintering, anemone-widening harmonies
Of the architectonic-misting horizon in the marigold-
Arching wombs of my silver-incarnate, vernal-perfecting soul

I am the mantra-dappled spirit of the sunset-affirming
Cathedral knowing that there is no divine presence
Beyond the sibylline-pallid, Lindisfarne-darkening walls
That god is only a marsh-chasmed, Aeolian-entranced figment
Of the grey-layered, astral-labyrinthine dust

I am a spherical-latticed odyssey of wisteria-morphine,
Jade-iridescent silences of a hundred Sevres-lavender mandalas
Waiting to be reborn in Florentine-wise cascades of grail-
Leavening suns transforming poplar-scented pain into orphic-
Almandine breaths of Castle Howard-exalting light.

## ACROSS THE SEA OF GALILEE

I spill luminous whispers of time across the sea of Galilee
Coral-turquoise dusks of time transmuting
Rainbow-swelling winds in altar-splaying fingers of
    onyx-pale light
Seeking lavender arbors of architrave-languishing truths,

I weave Babel silences of Delft-blue communion gardens
In velvet-purple euphonies of motionless, precipitous
    mill-echoes,
Twilight adorations of immaculate silver breezes
Seeking blue-neon crosses of Eden-phosphorescent stars

In silent eaves of ineradicable faith and bronze-foam rosaries,
Epitaphs of ancient souls in cyclamen mirrors
Of Gemini-wandering dawns, seeking internal harmonies
In chrysalis-ascending nocturnes of amaryllis-Aegean dreams.

# I Opened a Star

I opened a star
And found a piece of time
A piece of orange-helixed time
A foundling piece of time
Lost by Mercury, dispersed by Minerva,
Forgotten by God—waiting for the sea,
Waiting for fragile-listening epitaphs of frost-shafted horizons,
Waiting for mandrake-dusk elixirs of salmon-columbine light;

I opened a star and found
A piece of cyclamen-lavishing time,
Of calyx-chastening, solstice-surging time
Diffusing light in Magdalene carnation-arpeggios,
A piece of morning spinning summer ivories
Of words in moon-compassed pools of amphibrach lilies
Suspending light in orphic-trellised, harp-satyred dominions;

I opened a star
And found a piece of time
Along the Sargasso edge of lavender-madrigal twilight
Lost from chamomile-lace wings of soft-gusting angels
Shaping Babel crocuses into soft-broken, maroon-thistled
Silhouettes of saffron-desolate tears,
A piece of endless, gelatinous, immortal time
Waiting for prophesies of sunflower dreams,
Healing fissures of auroral-lemon silences.

## SHAPING THE FIGURES OF THE DANCE

A dance of crystalline-jasmine waves across the platinum-
   lambent shore of eternity
A dance of twelve Sidha karya offerings across an iris-
   consecrating lake of fallow lightning
A dance of twelve violins across an allegretto-discoursing
   pastiche of sforzando-pendulous unicorns
A dance of twelve snapdragons across a translucent chime of
   palomar-garlanding light
A dance of twelve breezes across a crimson-diapason meadow
   of Florentine-onyx oases
A dance of twelve Artemisian-lavender, Eroica-perpetuating
   lines sheltering the green-apsed, mirabelle-chastening divine
   eye
I am the Degas-calligraphic, solstice-winding soul
   of the universe shaping the figures of the dance
      in lotus-furrowed mirrors of grail-sceptered
         silences and tiffany-amber suns.

# A Salmon-Shadowed Figure

A salmon-shadowed figure entering the mist-leavening,
Fjord-softening waters of the talisman-margined forest-lake
Ascending the threshold aura of the divine
In his own damask-serene, porcelain-templed mind
Moving on mandala-dewed tremors towards the adamanthine-
Crimson, saffron-gloaming source of Pythian-oak,
Cypress-embering sublimity, an orphic-halcyon creator
Shaping abbey-crystalline scansions and legato-eternal
Silences of the dusk-blooming horizon in pristine-
Luminous solitudes of moist-cisalpine infinity;

A phoenix-conceiving creator among his catacomb-staved
Moor-chimes carving dove-Cistercian knells of amber-
Rolling Pleiades on autumn-aspen monoliths of cervical-
Saturated scarecrows, filling promontory spells
With sandstone epitaphs of dactylic-liminal light
Breaking fragile-emerald mirrors of time on willow-
Splashing vagaries of Rehoboth-hieratic barrow-dreams,
A silmarillion-serene composer shaping Rhadamanthus
Absolutions from tidal wisps of summer-amoebae dreams
Calling crescent-counterpaned, dawn-veined clouds
Into august-lavender lagoons of calyx-cascading,
Maple-webbed light
Calling the sea home to his Thames-silent, moss-
Cadenced shore of twilight immortality.

## PILASTERS OF SOFT-DEWED OMNIPOTENCE

As the Scythian-majestic towers rise through the Maia-
Empyrean mists the silence of the apocalypse peals
Across the sable-merlined wind the moss-darkened clouds
Reappear and disperse in crimson-apertured cycles
Like Gunterstein-furrowing thoughts in linden-incurable
Panoplies of moor-gleaming, auburn-chasmed light
Corinthian-pinioned pilasters of soft-dewed omnipotence
Surging through amorphous-duned blizzards of white-cairned
Breezes shaping immaculate dreams of golden-veined
Pallors on lonely bridges of Palladian-wise intensity
Two figures shaping contemplative, mercurial radiances
With cypress-cascading horizons touching the sun
Through the amber-knolled haze in amethyst-enamelled
Pyres of orange-diapason light carving time
On Weltschmerz-measureless distances of Chatsworth-
    burgeoning
Streams as the diamond-lintelled meridian-tears conceive
The oracular destiny of the magenta-effusive sky
In rushing, seething billows of Geneva-equinoctial,
Fountains-whispering light the sea becomes a crystalline
Inflection breaking into a thousand angles of tempest-woven
Sighs dissolving into myriad masks of Aeolian-lyred
Shells reshaping the sun in onyx-tendrilled windmills
Of lily-gloaming, amaranth-centering light.

## ACROSS ARCADIAN MEADOWS

When a silent-sublime creator walks across
Arcadian-liminal meadows of marble-gentian light
She lures perpetual-sage time away from mortality
And shapes transience into russet-steepled mists
Of immutable-soaring skylarks and eglantine-fervent,
    muse-blossoming paradise

When an amaranth-floating creator permeates the sky
With cypress-roaming solitudes and emerald-adamanthine
Chimes of Hermes-shadowed towers he opens the translucent
Folds of eternity in saffron-gloaming epiphanies
Of cosmic-pensive, willow-germinating paean-harmonies;

An orphic-chrysalis heart of sapphire-liberating,
Helicon-preserving vales and Byzantine-resonant,
Stonehenge-articulate magnanimity shaping tiara-poised
Silhouettes of time in lavender-infallible, madrigal-
Glowing silences emanating from porcelain-meadowed,
Crimson-ripening light-vases,
A divine-conceiving heart of Parnassus-revolving
Harmonies guiding lost souls to lily-cascading, azure-
Binding sanctuaries of Gautama-burgeoning, emerald-feeling
Light.

# THE SOUL OF THE DANCE II

We are the soul of the dance
In hexagonal-coloratura symmetries
   of magenta-silicon mezzotints
We are the Shiva-culminating soul
Of the dance in melisma-curving
   nebulae of jasmine-cresting,
      panorama-mazed wisdom
We are the soul of the dance
In supple-aquamarine fantasies
   of auroral-descending light
We are the soul of eternity shaping
The willow-pulsing horizon
   in Tchaikovsky-vaned synergies of light

We are the soul of the dance
In dynastic-silken rhythms of marigold-
Christening radiances we are the soul of the dance
In Michelangelo-gloaming, andante-flowing waves
Of chiaroscuro-leavening, albemarle-deepening light
We are the soul of the dance in lily-
   cascading, porcelain-ripening cadences
     of orphic-resurrecting, cypress-spanning
       Artemisian mysteries

We are the soul of the twilight-breathing wind
Healing the mistral-glazed wounds of mortality
In azure-masqued, anemone-luminescent silences
   Of Promethean-lyred, acanthus-concentric
     Emanations reuniting Adonis-lingering,
       Lily-pulsating intuitions with the crescent-
Sage, divine-opalescent dawn of eternity

# A Dance of Twelve Souls

A dance of twelve goldenrod-tasseled trees
   along a palomar-divine lake of Aeolian-raising
      purple-thistle-lulls

A dance of twelve loggia-bells on a chamomile-
   pervading sea of Aphrodite-crimson light

A dance of twelve Olana-sunset silences
   on a Pleiades-marble reverie of willow-profound,
      Isis-shrining cloud-truths

A dance of twelve serpentine-weaving shadows
   along a heath-misting path of Matterhorn-lonely,
      maze-astered head-stones

A dance of twelve mandrake-converting exiles
   of cruciform-sage, Promethean-spiring light

A dance of twelve myrrh-solemn portals
   around a genesis-revealing, merivale-sacred apotheosis
      of cypress-winding, dusk-autumn light

A dance of twelve orchid-winds across a Gemini-
   architraved meadow of petunia-alabaster,
      apricot-rhythmed light

A dance of twelve orange-topaz day-lilies
   before the mosaic-singing, aquamarine-
      transmuting apocalypse

A dance of twelve crystalline-pallid whirlpools
  of megalithic-arching light on andromeda-
    porcelain hexagons of russet-yellow-undulating
      infinity

A dance of twelve souls of Apollonian magnanimity
  given freely, joyously, lovingly
    to a world wrapped in intolerant imperfections

A dance of twelve Gautama-spacious souls
  of rainbow-surging, Rembrandt-veined melodies
    transmuting time in amber-gyred affinities
      of resonant-yellow, onyx-diagonal reflections

A dance of twelve pomegranate-horizoned soul-voices
  shaping the Adriatic-runed edge of time
    in philomel-intuitions and anemone-encompassing
      sighs of Easter-stamened, Ravenna-moist solitudes

## ODYSSEY-PALE TEARS

A Hermes-lonely, logos-inviolable wanderer staring
Across the Atlantic-crepuscular cove in an indigo-
Cascading cloud of jonquil-sacramental reveries
Watching for the ambrosia-chanting ocean
To divide in a maroon-tempest zodiac of seagull-almandine
Echoes shaping ibis-cracked graves in purple-alabaster
Cylinders of crescent-sabbath light soaring ancient-kylix
Whispers of cemetery-mandolin dreams across pale-swollen,
Grain-jaundiced headstones along the Gemini-vaulting,
Amen-raising horizon;

Odyssey-pale tears roll down his face
In cumulus-casting breaths of emerald-sated
Sculptures spilling time from Arcturus-fevered
Dreams onto the syrinx-wounded shore
Tears streaming dove-gelatinous tenderness
And sapphire-tympanum exodus across magi-
Vaulting harmonies of Arcadian-releasing,
Oleander-tolling rhythms tears swelling cinnabar-
Uranium spheres of megalithic, unfinished, crocus-
Mirroring light across dahlia-vascular, mimosa-
Pealing gardens of pine-radiant, soft-eternal hearts.

## A CERULEAN-ANCIENT CEREBRUM

I am the moss-primeval northside of a cemetery-apsed
Wall where only Brancusi-corniced dreams and kinetic-
Soaring reveries appear to appease the onyx-marrowed streams
Of iris-silent tears flowing from primordial-sepulchered eaves
Of my Merivale-gloaming heart where no one ever comes
Except the translucent-crippled soul to feed the heath-
Whispering swallows and the lavender-transomed ferns

I am a cerulean-ancient cerebrum of sycamore-bearing,
Zodiac-encompassing stones listening to the solitary-
Opulent zephyrs of amber-helixed, agate-chastening time
I am the fir-arching embodiment of Samothrace-liminal
Sadness hearing the glib, spangled words of the people
Going to church and knowing there is no god anywhere
Except the spherical-webbed soliloquies of dusk-gloaming,
Dawn-twittering mirrors.

# A FLOWER ON THE COFFIN

He stayed beside the coffin for hours
And days when she died feeling that death
Had struck him too and wondering at its strangeness
For never again as a mortal would he talk with her
Or look into her eyes knowing that they mirrored
His love, never again in all the eons and centuries
Of the world would he be with her except in spirit
And he wondered how a benevolent god could allow this
A stream of flowers bore the coffin to its final home
Where only haggard stones and dusty-windswept leaves
Remind of a brief interval of life and then vanish too
As he knelt upon the ground beside her grave prostrate
In grief and adoring anguish a vision rose upon his
Inner eye that there was no god at all a vision
As radiant and irreversible as the light of the conversion
Of St. Paul on the road to Damascus, and yet perhaps
There is a fragile-mitred heaven where dead souls wander
In labyrinthine contentment or astral-misting delight,
When the evening wind rushed across cemetery solitudes
In amber-veiled matrices of Botticelli-lambent light
He became one of the primrose-carving reveries
On the coffin and forever a phoenix-lonely,
Heliotrope-wandering soul.

# AMARANTH-EMULATING TREMORS OF ETERNITY

The only god is within us
Alone, furtive, mysterious
In its elfin-frail autonomy
Completing the self in amaryllis-veined
Harps of autumn-suffusing light
I listen to the silence of the snow
Speaking of divine-subterranean, emerald-
Vaulting shadows more lovely than
The ripening of Moselle-refulgent vines
I see endless footsteps in onyx-white stillness
Streaming in azalea-sentient circles towards
The Wartburg-pinioned, hibiscus-radiant center
Of the earth perpetuating the cedar-swelling
Exile of twilight tombs I feel the seraphic-
Laminating tranquillity of glacial-apsed
Wastelands of Caspian-shattered waves
I shape amaranth-emulating, Beethoven-iridescent
Tremors of eternity in honeysuckle-pulsing
Ravines of hermetic-moist, sage-encompassing
Dreams.

# Shaping the Gothic-Liminal Heart

I am a red-deepening, ark-translucent spiral
Of apocalyptic-white, Upton-vaned light
Shaping the amber-streaming, Gothic-liminal heart
Of the deluge-undulating universe in gladiolus-
Veined tones of meridian-nurturing, cherry-misting
Helixes and almandine-oval scars of serpentine-
Angled light I am the genesis-lavender,
Lily-enchanting wind redeeming astral-escutcheoned
Contours of diamond-expanding glades and magnolia-
Sentient, arabesque-metamorphosing graves
In architectonic-crystalline shadows permeating
The sun with the yellow-opalescent fragility
Of mortal-lacquered, primrose-gelatinous tears
I am an Aeolian-architraved whirlpool of primordial-
Crimson, andante-murmuring blossoms falling
In cairn-dewed, untamed dissonances on the wisteria-
Laced, mezzotint-paned abyss of blue-collapsing,
Candle-stoned spring.

## When Twilight Falls

When twilight falls along the shore
The seagulls cry against the waves
Nirvana parables of eternity
Cytherean whispers of forgotten graves

When darkness talks to silver-vertigo sands
Of Nietzsche and de Chirico
Phoenix-jade echoes swelling soft-crepuscular bands
Of onyx-bridled anemone dreams across

The journey of the old magi
Still travelling, drifting in time
Still searching for a lost omen
Of wisdom, a saffron-veined rosary of light,

When twilight falls against the edge
Of an old tavern, no one is there—
An agony of emptiness spills
Over her auburn-scattered hair.

# A FACE OF ANCIENT-PALOMAR DREAMS

A face of ancient-palomar, zodiac-cascading dreams
And grail-furrowed, Isis-wandering sadnesses
Creases the moist-enamelled, lintel-swelling sky
In kithara-glowing frescoes of Delphic-searching,
Gemini-crepuscular light, a magenta-solstice face
Of blue-mosaic whispers and pink-rotunda eyes
Softening the mortality of calico-glazed,
Chrysanthemum-dewed thresholds in dusk-tympanum
Eclogues of myrrh-gleaming, Cistercian-ethereal light
A face of Cain-muted, Lazarus-mantled exodus
At the jagged-saturn, rhododendron-scarred edge
Of the silicon-orange, Rheims-vaulting horizon
Radiating Pachelbel-crystalline incantations
Of apocalypse-spanning, ambrosia-weaving solitudes.

## What if God

What if God were a sanctuary of light,
A suffering of heaven, a furtive lament
Of seagulls shrieking exodus in sunset-desolate lagoons,
What if God were an echo
Of Stygian chimeras shedding pristine fires
Of sand-strained light across lapis lazuli
Corridors of marble-sculpted prisms,
What if God were a bronze pyre
Of primordial vigils shearing madrigal
Petals from frozen-crimson idols,
The path to Heaven lies through the heart

What if God were a stray filament of time
Leaning carelessly against a decaying, twilight barn
What if God were a dissolution of time,
A suspension of space in crimson-wired dreams
Of summer-barbed asters,
What if God were a cloistered refuge
For merciful souls and sad eyes,
The path to Heaven lies through the heart

What if God were a stone-sated echo
Of inner visions lost in teeming convergences
Of primal myths, tropical wildernesses,
What if God were a mirror
Broken and forgotten among cavernous ruins
By Promethean prophets, ephemeral yearnings,
What if God were an ancient dream
Of cypress-moated castles beyond the final edge
Of fragile-auburn layers of sunset horizons
Where Amazon-turquoise winds shape
Soft-fermenting omens of lost Caucasus waterfalls,
The path to Heaven lies through the heart

# A Syrinx-Trembling Ring

Somewhere after Armageddon among the twilight amplitudes
Of specter-sated ruins and Parthenon-marrowed oracles
A calliope-scented piece of marble-tendrilled parchment
Will flutter in gaunt-willow remembrance of the nativity,
Of Dionysian mysteries, and Shiva-conceiving shrines,
Lily-inviolate strands of fragile-evening Books of Hours
Among the hegira-embering clerestory-crucifixes scattered
With the mastaba-moist signature of leviathan-blue death
Olympian-kylix improvisations and Tillai-masqued
Incantations among the jade-sutured basilica-chains
    of frozen-fevered smiles
A syrinx-trembling ring of wind-stamened hieroglyphs
Will float odyssey-lyred pietà-diptychs over mantra-
Carillons estuaries of indigo-mullioned, pyrrhic-fluted
Despair with several, mandolin-haloed lines for a new
Beginning, secreting chrysalis-Ganges apparitions
Of phoenix-splintering, rainbow-metamorphosing dawns.

# THE ISENHEIM ALTARPIECE

Until the world understands the Isenheim Altarpiece
Nothing will change,
A crucifixion of hermetically painful silences and coronal
Dawns weeping seeds of panhellenic graces
Bearing the sins of the earth in pearl-stained tears
Of extraterrestrial wisdom, bearing the hope of the earth
In horizon-rainbow apostrophes of ancient-alluvial adorations,
The face of Rembrandt knows the immortality of sunflowers
In the solstice-ascending radiance of Atlantis-astered dreams
A timeless face of ethereally lonely wisdom
Only when Rembrandt shows Christ the sunflowers
The Chartres-empyrean, self-surpassing radiance
Of Van Gogh's flowers in endless saffron-stamened
Synergies of amaranth-helixed light
Will the seraphic-crystalline river of polyphonic
Diffusions begin to flow in odyssey-surging, toccata-
Amber echoes along the immortal edge of the Isenheim
    Altarpiece.

## THE EVENING CLOUDS

The gondola-reticulating clouds are the Cisalpine-
Endless, Newstead-exiled thoughts of a divine mind
Searching for the leviathan repose of tameless,
    Praxiteles tears,
The Hesperus-expressing clouds are the last mural-
Adoring reflections of a messiah-protean mind
Recasting its immortality in vermilion-webbed,
Pumice-fettered vortices of myrrh-glowing light
Sealing its Endymion-sheaved link with the sun
In an auburn-crystalline, Cyclades-converging beam
Of sublime-abalone, thorn-vaulting silences,
Dark-foaled tempietto-megaliths on the Nepal-
Twilight horizon congealing ancient wind-echoes
In labyrinthine-trembling mirrors of Eolian-
Dewed, silver-breathing light.

## AN ORANGE-DRYADIC SUN

An orange-dryadic sun thickens acacia memories
    Of light across arborealis silhouettes of time
As the ritual of life swelters in diastolic echoes
    Of decaying Mediterranean sands, waiting for the gust of
        wind
Coming out of a broken, bridge-shearing window-pane
    Scattering frail, everlasting presentiments of wisdom,

Of the wisdom of evanescence, into the universal
    Night of the soul, I condense time into thresholds
Of light, where the sea haunts the dawn
    In soft-lacquering haloes of pomegranate and
Jade absolutions, only the maroon-diffusing sunset
    Reveals the truth about the Amber-misting horizon.

# EROICA-MODULATING EPIPHANIES

Revelations of an Indus-whispering mind
Beyond basilica-mazed stone-rituals
And Byzantine-dusted sunset-meridians embracing
The Isis-deepening universe of dahlia-globed
Masks and poppy-murmuring light at the threshold
Of the brine-molten, compass-gleaning horizon
A Shiva-tidal incarnation of the spirit
Beyond time and history culminating in the flamingo-
Confessing wisdom of angelus-transmuting light
A mind of Thoth-dewed clouds
And coreopsis-germinating helixes
Of amber-tendering light which changes
And reshapes itself but cannot die
Transforming mortality into Eroica-modulating
Epiphanies of night-dissolving, marsh-
Golding grace, timeless chiaroscuro-effusions
Of windmill-evolving, saffron-asphodel light,
A mind shaping its spiritual permanence
In the aura of sublime-terraced autumn-icons
Of crystalline-surging, Delphic-eaved sunset-moors
And blue-vaulting, Tintern-sage harmonies
Of the fermata-ribboned, crimson-vespered west wind.

# THE ANGELS OF THE ANNUNCIATION

The angels of the annunciation
Only reappear when the amaranth-blue,
Chrysanthemum-consecrating wind rustles softly
Through immaculate-jade, porcelain-blossoming birches
And when dusk-perfecting, menhir-lambent aureoles
Of late-afternoon wind-knells convene
The Mnemosyne-tenoned renascence of acacia-
Numinous, pine-sceptered silences,
The angels recasting time
In El Greco-luminous calligraphies
Of lily-arching, rune-chasmed voices
And dithyrambic-willow dreams of amethyst-hexagonal,
Piranesi-spiraling domes of liminal-apertured light,
Saffron-rising, Delft-winged angels reshaping
Empyrean intuitions of ineffable, Bernini-agape
Joy in the auburn-delicate, pomegranate-scented
Opulence of the nativity and in unicorn-sheaved
Prisms of orchid-weaving, amber-purifying timelessness.

## SAVING THE DREAMS OF HERMES

There was a traveler on the silent road
Who walked alone for miles and acacia-endless
Miles where few would dare to tread and weep
He walked away inevitably from the lichen-darkened
Vanities and orchid-masked corruptions of civilized
Illusions to the sacred forest where a lapis lazuli-
Haunted, marble-ringed castle lay upon the primeval
Heart of Nature, he strode through the laurel-
Darkening hallows of time-fettered vapors where
Only sable-ewered carrion and red-shrouded ghosts
Rise from the mistral air, they touched him not,
They let him pass as if they knew of his coming,
As if his presence were foreordained by raven-
Billowing silences, as if a spectacle of amber-
Furrowed flames illumined his inner way, the lonely
Traveler came upon the castle with the mantra-chiming,
Janus-labyrinthine door exuding pale-golden phantasma
Of philomel-mourning moor-gleams, he became a Lethe-
Sceptered resonance of diamond-effulgent light saving
The dreams of the horizon in willow-lingering chalices
Of sublime-pulsing tempests in his equinoctial-serene
Castle saving the dreams of Osiris, Athena, and Hermes
In the wreath-templed glooms and alabaster-mazed reveries
Of his Titian-effusive heart—once every thousand years
A solitary traveler knows the road to eternity
In the Salisbury-emerald profundity of his damask-
Shattered, saffron-germinating, agape-flowing soul.

## OF AMSTEL-VANED SOLITUDES

In the pomegranate-dewed, ethereal-gray shadow
Of the estuary-veined windmill rises a margrave-solstice
Figure endowed with Elysian-tendrilled eternity
By amber-kinetic blooms of ancient-Bavo winds and blue-
Tempest peals of Catskill-spiring willow-truths
Dispersing Promethean-tessera hymns of architectonic-
Primeval isolation, untouched by Taormina-fertile
Rivulets of vain, hourglass rituals, creating the pyramid-
Sage sublimity of sail-dissolving, saffron-tremulous
Timelessness in Hyperion-discoursing silences of cobalt-
Mediating, Amstel-vaned solitudes.

# The Poem

The poem is a fragile silence
Where the sky meets the sea
In an enchanted moment
Of ethereal dreams and unvanquished epiphanies,

The poem is a soft-amber vision
Of pallid, pendulous augurs of eternity,
A sanctuary of self-overcoming Promethean rituals,
An immortal wound of Apollonian light,

The poem is a place where the poet
Can breathe freely, fully,
And search for truth and faith
Vitally beyond mortality;

The poem is a voice seething broken-chiming
Rivulets of Munch echoes across dusk-sibilant margins
Of alabaster-phoenix, Goya-solstice dreams,

A voice beyond aberrant-apsed amplitudes
And sinewy-promising sabbaths, lifting
The sea from soft-embered estuaries

Of prodigal time, a voice transmuting seasons
Into inviolate insinuations of pyramid-dawns
And helix-running sand-graces,

A voice beyond the remembrance of time
Beyond chrysalis-surpassing knells, a voice
Calling quietly in sapphire-palladium repose.

# A Mist of Marigold-Intuitive Communions

When the moon shapes the heart of the cypress
In magenta-veined blooms of light a double rainbow
Rises from the sea in Cythere-streaming reflections
Of Pleiades-amber suns and eglantine-prophetic resonances
Of lilac-permeating, Cassandra-evolving wisdom
A primrose-leavening deluge of angel-traversing light
Opens the stone-lichened doors of the ancient temple
Closed for centuries an acacia-numinous mist of marigold-
Intuitive communions creates the Atlantis-liminal soul
Of the Castalian-rhythmed horizon in mandrake-gloaming,
Eleusinian-flowing diasporas of pink-amaryllis, Delphic-
Weaving eternities.

# A Millennial-Sacred Grove

A millennial-sacred grove where the Florentine-magenta
Confluence of the light of four porcelain-sage vases
Is the emerald-astered soul of eternity

A vase of gladiolus-conceiving, purple-iridescent muses
Receding into dove-interminable distances of pallid-
Glowing, Renoir-immaculate silences

A vase of piazza-feverish solitudes decaying into orange-
Metaphysical shells of crystalline-fertile, Fontainebleau-
Exalting light

A vase of Vermeer-listening mirrors arching into
Petrified-combing obelisks of Cassandra-elegant shadows

A vase of diachronic-lemon astral-harps animating
The sea in amphora-infinite mobiles of sphinx-hermetic,
Lunar-weeping light

A sacred-lavender grove where the diffusion of the light
Of melancholy-jade haloes of cypress-germinating,
Dusk-embalming statues is the renascence-breathing soul
Of Blickling-effulgent eternity.

# I Am a Goldau-Misting Tapestry

I am a Goldau-misting, Oxburgh-sacred tapestry
Of unicorn-dreaming, Elysian-tendrilled snow-aureoles
Shaping the first day of spring in cypress-radiant
Cantatas of pearl-shadowed, onyx-soaring synergies
Sealing the flux of time in phoenix-dewed silences
Of Lyndhurst-exalting, velvet-trembling light
I am the hyacinth-weaving, amaranth-diapason heart
Of the Gobelin-streaming, Pythian-veined wind
Carving apocalyptic-jade blossoms of magenta-perfecting
Genesis on amaryllis-chiming, marble-gloaming mirrors.

## SELF-TRANSFORMATION

I waited by the sea for the apparition
To emerge from heliotrope-magenta waves
I waited to behold the golden-dewed chalice
In his turquoise-ewered hands
And as he came upon the shore
The waves drove tempestuous-lintelled cries
Across the sands towards emerald-sated skies
And as he held the Hever-vestal chalice
Over the Aeolian-moist reveries an auburn-
Tendrilled sunset-gleam arose from indigo-
Spectral clouds to pierce the shining vortex
And as they touched the old world ceased to be
A deluge of crimson-mantled, cedar-haloed light
Vanquished the semblance of a world and created
A new arabesque-conceiving tapestry of life
The apparition became the new sun and I became
The sea along the amaranth-templed shore where
Penshurst-arching silences share onyx-scrolled
Divinations of sacred time with melancholy-
Raptured sighs of seagull-wandering, iris-yearning
Solitudes and the chalice became the mantra-pulsing
Horizon where sibylline-veiled eternity meets
The Arcadian-possessing pause of Pleiades-curving
Infinity.

# I Am the Rubens-Panelled Soul

In the azalea-vaulted corridors of the east cloister
Linger marble-veined memories of ancient-madrigal silences
A Tudor-domed mantlepiece of rainbow-persisting arabesques
Exudes hyacinth-parabled, Vishnu-apsed voices
Of oaken-pilastered, Gemini-lyred dreams
Rose-trellised crosses perceive the seraphic-misting flux
Of the sable-cairned dance in Vesuvius-rustling flames
Of mandrake-dewed, golden-diaphanous elixirs
I am the Rubens-panelled, porcelain-blossoming soul
Of the zephyr-carving, astral-dawning gallery
Restoring the vermilion-architraved, obelia-murmuring
Euphonies of the gargantuan-chasmed manorial halls
In ruby-decaying excrescences of Godington-jonquil light
In auburn-elusive incarnations of Blenheim-ethereal,
Fugal-pristine mirrors.

## The Soul of the Universe

I am the soul of the universe
Collecting Gautama-fragile sadnesses in my soul
Gathering Pythian-white clouds of melancholy
Sagacity in the dusk-compassionate expanse
Of my Vedic-whispering soul
Shaping the hope of the world
In amber-gloaming, acacia-numinous timelessnesses
Of my Bernini-sceptered, lily-conceiving soul
Perpetuating Snowdonia-cresting, delphinium-
Frescoed resonances of saffron-evolving, azure-
Unvanquished trinities of Aphrodite-shrining light

I am the soul of the universe
Integrating divine-opalescent angles of sea-composing
Harmonies with muse-weaving calyxes
Of late-afternoon, millenial-astered horizons
Pervading the Thoth-sheaved longevity
Of alchemistic meridians with chrysalis-luminescent
Tonalities of pine-cosmic evening-silences
Shaping the Giverny-flowing, wisteria-lavender
Timelessness of pristine-adamanthine forests
In Promethean-sage, amaryllis-halcyon reveries
Of orchid-twilight memories of Friedrich-altared,
Magenta-soaring eternity

I am the soul of the universe
Consecrating cyclical convergences of camellia-
Blossoming, Jura-trembling thresholds
In Geneva-columbine incantations of Florentine-
Vaulting, Elysian-perfecting cloud-hearts
Revealing rainbow-diastolic, Apollonian-pure
Diffusions of the sublime-luminescent, helicon-
Serene soul of Nature

I am the soul of the universe
Saving autumnal-megalithic suns and ancient-
Madrigal moons from the whirlpools of time
In Harlaxton-veined dawns of my diamond-lintelled,
Marigold-diapason soul
Embracing the soul of the sea
With mimosa-helixed, sapphire-iridescent sunset-winds
Of my amaranth-resurrecting, Orpheus-pulsing soul.

# I Am the Soul of the Twilight

I am the Sebastian-embering soul of the wisteria-
Rustling twilight sealing mortality in crystalline-
Pinioned globes of Isis-soaring, Atlas-seething light
I am the honeysuckle-luminescent soul of the zodiac-evolving
Twilight shaping mausoleum-pallid hearts in alabaster-red-
    arpeggios
Of salmon-androgynous, pollen-procreating silences

I am the primrose-diffusing soul of the Zarathustra-
Cadenced evening wandering through margrave-vaulting,
Emerald-panelled halls echoing the cosmic-astral serenity
Of jasmine-endless, rainbow-perpetuating solitudes
In the silver-marrowed depths of my orchid-stained,
Nepenthe-melodious soul I transform Castle Howard-effulgent,
Heliotrope-mazed silences of vesper-astered, hexagonal-
Misting galleries abandoned by mortal touch into self-
Germinating suns of rhapsodic-liminal, Cyclades-effusive
Light.

# THE APOLLONIAN-SAGE BRIDGE

I am the voice of the Mozart-soaring light
Shaping chamomile-leavening, acropolis-veined petals
Into almandine-eclectic suns of Michelangelo-gloaming
   eternity

I am the silence of the Grieg-misting darkness
Shaping cairn-willowed eaves of tiara-masked
Radiances into Böcklin-mitred isles of Hades-astered moons

I am the veil of the Picasso-horizoned morning
Transforming crimson-globed spaces of lavender-
Vestal light into Isis-effulgent melodies
Of poppy-weaving, amber-helixed dreams

I am the jonquil-ringed, Apollonian-sage bridge
Of Rhadamanthus-echoing, emerald-pilastered
Twilight connecting life and death in pink-
Ethereal, Elysian-tendrilled seas of Beethoven-
Luminescent, lily-diapason cherry blossoms.

## I Am an Amber-Prophetic Stone

I am a madonna-wise piece of andante-liminal stone
Creating Gothic-torrential, Marmorsaal-radiant manor-
Aureoles consecrating silver-encircling silences
Of hyacinth-spiritual shadows in stained-glass triptychs
Of phoenix-empyrean mazes waiting for the melisma-
Spinning evening sun to touch zodiac-destined, wisteria-
Grottoed leaves around me in a crimson-apsed ferment
Of Neuschwanstein-soaring solitudes

I am an amber-prophetic stone speaking in the dusk-
Gloaming tones of porcelain-twilight, sunflower-yearning
Paradise I am the Turner-eloquent soul of the jonquil-
Glorifying chandelier encompassing the sacred-
Illuminating profundity of the ancient-timbered,
Dynastic-proportioned aura in universe-spanning
Thresholds of Harlaxton-magnanimous, amaranth-
Effulgent space

I am an Amsterdam-vaned stone washed by nocturne-soft
Horizons sealing the reveries of the lotus-shaping moat
In crescent-dewed silhouettes of astral-corniced time
I am a diadem-templed stone breathing Elysian-tendrilled
Intimations of heliotrope-swirling light over the deluge-
Flickering fields and mandolin-cairned meadows
I am a Delft-pealing stone weaving the acropolis-saving
Silences of the asphodel-helixed wind in pomegranate-
Leavening mirrors of Ruisdael-lambent, acanthus-golden light.

# THE LIGHT OF THE DANCE

# THE LIGHT OF THE DANCE

The morning trees dance pearl-cusped ballets
Of albemarle-moist, jasmine-floating light
Along juniper-gusting preludes of mauve-electric
Dusks the morning trees perceive the heart
Of the dawn in a cypress-lintelled pool of lavender-
Raising light healing the wounds of labyrinthine-
Angled darkness in auburn-crystalline, polonaise-
Resonating harmonies of empyrean-solitary words
In Goldau-exalting convergences of Alhambra-arborealis-
    philomel-ripples

The morning trees carve the emerald-lyred, melisma-
    immaculate
Intimations of the day on the mazurka-vocative, marigold-
Chastening edge of the horizon in hierophant-crimson,
    Atlantis-
Engulfing vortices of Gemini-tentacled light
Heron-gnostic signs of pristine-orphic sanctuaries
Of timelessness foretelling the inevitable decline
Of god-centered mortality in clover-weaving calyxes
Of luminescent-gesturing, alpine-mazed infinities
In moonlight-loosening synergies of andante-cascading,
Cerulean-congealing aureoles

Listen to the music of the light with the harp-singing,
Ambrosia-pulsing vision of your saffron-numinous inner soul
The light of the dance is the music of eternity.

## OF PHOENIX-DEWED CONSTELLATIONS

A capriccio-pulsating pool of obelia-blossoming,
Terpsichore-poised light shaping the nightingale-confessing,
Angelus-weaving sky in dusk-emerald triptychs of muslin-
Terraced stone-echoes and Llanberis-sacred liminal-sighs
Of hyacinth-chastening, Venetian-exiled dreams conceiving
Its own silver-immaculate wisdom in the incarnate radiance
Of pink-leavening zephyrs enclosed in sea-revolving
    hieroglyphs
Of orchid-soaring, Everest-tendering light transforming
The dark-thorned ravages of time in phoenix-dewed
    constellations
Of clover-pinioned, eglantine-murmuring eyes redeeming
Legato-hermetic silences in pyramid-astered, Aeolian-
    autumnal tears.

# THE THRESHOLD-WIND

In the lavender-onyx rustling of the late-afternoon
Threshold-wind I hear ancient-Ganges soliloquies
Of hydrangea-blue, sapphire-meridian light shaping
Thames-burgeoning annunciations of saffron-diapason,
Ring-corniced light in porcelain-templed
Calligraphies of luminous-helixed wisdom

In the mandala-leavening threshold-wind
I hear Stygian-white prayers of the Protean divine
Spilling pink-tempera suns across Amen-martyred
Refractions of Nile-auburn light murmuring nightingale-
Architectonic prophesies of Athena-wandering dreams
On delta-marlin covenants of galvanic-altared sand-dews

In the amaranth-moist threshold-wind I touch the
    Apollonian-
Crimson, muse-weaving source of poetry, of all eternal-
Shrouded, poinsettia-scrolled words, and alcaic-
Extraterrestrial voices in silver-oracular, Rhine-deepening
Reflections of divine-crepuscular, marble-surging silences

The dusk-tempest threshold-wind reveals the angel-healing,
Marigold-communing secrets of the myrtle-blessed, palladium-
Megalithic bridge in Michelangelo-incarnate breaths
Of tidal-infusing beings creating the mosaic-spinning
Soul of the paradise-confessing universe from oasis-pristine
Aureoles of Aegean-amaryllis, conch-ribboned light.

# A New Jersey Sunset

On a road in the Elysian-trembling, Osiris-leavening
Epoch between Princeton and Barnegat Bay
I entered a Church-vaulting sunset of Euganean proportions
A twilight vision of endless-gelatinous, cenotaph-porous
Eternity in carmine-burgeoning, astral-miranda echoes
Of manna-orange, ancient-timbered horizons
For a prolonged timeless moment I was in the Delphic-
Sunset vortex rising on purple-wandering helixes
Of alabaster-counterpaned light on a solitary-ripening chord
Of pink-tempera horizon somewhere in the heart
Of a savannah-whorled tropical-universe gazing
At a towering Amazon-balalaika waterfall
In pristine syllables of orchid-lavender oracles

I breathed in the andante-lavender fragrance
Of an Hippocrene-dewed flower shaping my soul
In diastolic-amber peals of the blossom of eternity,
I saw the architectonic murmurs of hidden kelp-valleys
Of radiolarian light shaping sonar-furrowing satellites
Of island-clustering, tangerine-dryadic winds,
I heard the heart of God beating on onyx-soft tremors
Of cinnabar-jade leaves breathing diamond-gloaming
    capillaries
Of white-cypress light into kithara-apsed margins of eternity.

# THE ANEMONE-GREEN EYES OF EVENING

I watch the anemone-green eyes of evening
Convene stray filaments of auburn-burgeoning
Time in Delft-wandering oracles of willow-
Sapphire breezes along the purple-stamened
Edge of the lily-misting, poplar-molten lake,

Softly germinating waves in cosmic memories
Of ancient-lavender silences and cinnabar-vellum
Marsh-blooms creating Schleswig-jade helixes
Of acropolis-leavening, kithara-threshing light,

Angular-warm tremors of eternity rippling
Portinari-frail surfaces in crystal-engraving
Murmurs of algae-elusive obelisks, shaping
Ochre-glowing time in cathedral-acanthus nocturnes
Of amaryllis-palomar, Lucerne-hermetic wisdom.

# The Home of the Butterflies

The home of the butterflies
Is an emerald-hyacinth pool of Promethean-
Boundless light encompassing red-flaming
Trees of willow-gentian eyes

The home of the butterflies
Is an alpine-pinnacled dance of spring
A wisteria-crying nostalgia for the silence
Of the infinite for the sound of alpha-
Interwoven, glass-dewed harmonies

The home of the butterflies
Is a nightingale-epiphanic constellation
Of crystalline-silver, marble-veined spaces
A simultaneity of sun and moon
Where pearl-arching empires of seraphic-
Liminal light congeal in amaranth-gloaming mirrors

The home of the butterflies
Is an astral-tendrilled reverie
Of Apollonian-onyx unities
An orange-jade-streaming veil
Of tympanum-sceptered, lily-altared light

A Castalian-veined intuition of anemone-
Widening light where the helicon-sentient
Clouds fold time in albemarle-soaring
Rivulets of daemon-eclectic, Nile-glazed
Timelessness where the soul becomes a lunar-
Webbed chrysanthemum of pyramid-expanding
Eternity

A Protean-autumnal silence of hermetic-
Dreaming, horizon-marrowed light where
The souls of twilight-amber valences
Convene the iris-germinating, jasmine-
Permeating hearts of the odyssey-saving
Universe.

# Two Monarchs

Two small monarchs in the threshold tonality
Of Wessex-streaming, apocalyptic-red strands
Of pearl-carving light among Bosch-stained rushes
And indigo-primeval canopies of slate-onyx time,
Two monarchs on the edge of an Egeskov-silent brook
Molding marble-orange petals of light in gentian-
Black furrows of poppy-consuming weir-reveries,
A monarch transforming Himalayan time
Into cypress-winnowing fibers of fluorescent-apsed moss
A monarch shaping Alsen time
Into saffron epitaphs of immortal-scented sunflowers,
Two fragile-diapason monarchs gracefully crossing
Into soft-cinnabar megaliths of ancient cathedral-
Voices and purple-enameled flames of eternity
And back again to the lily-spawning, marsh-vaulting horizon.

# Twilight Invocations of Dusk-Mourning Beauty

Let the soul of the sea shape your soul
In Castalian-blossoming tremors of silver-
Crystalline eternity in the aura of gladiolus-
Perpetuating, mural-seraphic silences
The clocks are transmuted into crimson-effulgent
Chalices of Etretat-blue light

Let the soul of the sky shape your soul
In Andes-streaming reflections of jade-haunted
Moons in the aura of lighthouse-Nepenthe reveries
The pendulums are transformed into mountain-liberating
Angels converging softly in the alcaic-vaulting
Hearts of lily-onyx suns

Let the soul of the earth shape your soul
In Renoir-vermilion trilogies of rose-cream ripples
Existing only for the sensuousness of their own
Inner light in the aura of Luxor-burgeoning
Modulations apocalyptic-tensile rhythms fade
Into lapis lazuli-breathing, poppy-veined mirrors
Of rainbow-tentacled, Orangerie-sunset light

Let the soul of the divine shape your soul
In Chartres-enchanted nocturnes of Psyche-fevered,
Amaryllis-glistening light in the aura of Thames-
Echoing twilight-invocations of dusk-mourning beauty
The hourglasses vanish in Venus-sapphire chimes
Of Norham-pristine, nightingale-hermetic light.

## Let the Soul of Nature Be Your Soul

Let the vast-meadowed fragrance of amber-ethereal
Poppy-truths lull you to sleep in Elysian fields
Of phantasmal-pale cloud-silences, let the blue-seeking
Solitude absorb your soul in jade-sated infinity
Let the soul of Nature be your soul
Let it guide your life in concentric-evolving
    circles of saffron-diapason light
Let it enchant your soul in Arcadian-moist
    rhythms of violet-curving moor-spells
When the clock on the mantlepiece of God
    runs down it is only the artist who revives
        the flow of eternity in Pleiades-divine harmonies
            of pristine-gesturing, lunar-webbed light,

Let the soul of Nature fill your soul
With amorphous-sentient, mantra-soaring tremors
Of eternity with Petworth-incandescent revolutions
    of tessera-red, Eden-templed clouds
Let the soul of Nature fill your soul
With Thoth-preserving radiances of marigold-liminal,
Emerald-pledging light with fiery-celestial adorations
Of earth-trancing, white-animating estuary-plumes
When the festival-clock in the eye
Of the divinity fails it is only the poet
Of autumn-perpetuating twilight who will save
The sunset-gloaming luminescence of eternity,

Let the soul of Nature be your soul
In azure-dewed, Abydos-deepening melodies
Of honeysuckle-glistening, Utenwarf-echoing light
Let the soul of Nature be your soul
In nightingale-profound dreams of pristine-carmine,
Myrtle-folding mirrors and Endymion-ringed reveries
Of calyx-conceiving, yellow-gyrating light
When the maenad-stone clock collapses
In the crimson-fulfilling waves it is only the artist,
The poet, the dancer who saves the world
In a litany-diffusing, rainbow-perfecting cascade
Uniting light and color in primordial-sage,
Nocturne-flaming harmonies transposing mortality
Into flawless reflections of the Geneva-saffron,
Cerulean-expanding vortex of infinity
Transcending time in acropolis-discoursing
Inner sunrises of inestimable longing
And allegro-spinning, platinum-soaring light.

# A MAYA-PURPLE FLOWER

The branch of a plum tree extends its minuet-compassing eyes
On chrysanthemum-dewed silences into the almond-
    blossoming
Heart of the silver-crepuscular sea of longevity

A maya-purple flower of dawn-vernal, violin-pleated light
Binding the sky with magenta-pastel murmurs
Of Luxembourg-spiring garland-cadenzas

A rondo-venerating tendril creating nightshade-
Humming horizons of Thames-spectral light
In staccato-embroidered dreams of yellow-
Impassioned melodic-resolutions

A lento-textured bloom of gladiolus-ethereal,
Lavender-suave light scattering time
In Delft-curving streams of larkspur-compassionate,
Muse-inflecting words

A sapphire-reflective veil of amaryllis-muraled light
Sealing time in delphinium-tendrilled frescoes
Of contrapuntal-pinioned arabesques shaping timelessness
In Apollonian-soaring, dusk-blooming hearts
Of dithyramb-illuminating, pine-gloaming silences.

# THE DIVINATIONS OF THE WIND

Listen to the divinations of the wind in dusk-spiritual
Scherzos of Elgin-centrifugal light, let the wind fill
Your soul with diaphanous-white, heron-innocent stamen-
Odes of diadem-effervescent, Lanhydrock-glistening light,
The clouds are the madrigal-pristine, windmill-illuminating
Hearts of divine spirits evolving the earth, rising,
And wandering across Promethean-spanning, andante-
     widening
Horizons, searching for renaissance-mazed reflections
Of their eternal home
Let the wind shape your soul in calyx-gloaming wisps
Of emerald-germinating, Stourhead-rapturing light
Let the wind seep into the innermost depths of your spirit
Minuet-serene, syrinx-ethereal tremors of chrysalis-amber
Eternity as the night permeates the sky in millenial-astered
Vicissitudes of marigold-diapason, Atlantis-pulsing shadows.

## MOTHER NATURE

On a lily-bathing star of moist-apocryphal light
She waits for crescent-almondine echoes of iris-
Madrigal suns

In a silent corner of Stonehenge-auburn fields
She waits for phoenix-sceptered footsteps of grail-
Billowing exodus shaping the wind
In pristine-marigold asters of delta-germinating
Truths

Along the zodiac-lavender horizon
She waits on a saffron-gloaming butterfly-dream
Of amaryllis-jade light

In half-forgotten, Nepal-whispering omens
Of Olana winds she weaves carmine-crescent spells
And palladium smiles of porcelain-calyx swans
On magenta-architraved haloes of soft-decaying time.

# The Pool of Water Lilies

The empyrean-solitary pool of water lilies above time
Floating marigold-lyred aureoles over diastolic-trembling
Labyrinths beyond dawn-sceptered knells of cerulean-jade
Oracles and silicon-sunset silences of Vedic-warm rainbows
Beyond Hera-magenta arbors of delta-winged larkspur
And crescent-blue, Alhambra-misting iris-valences
Cassandra-evolving, oasis-embalming visions of diaphanous-
Pearl echoes spawning pink-anemone, palladium-soft breaths
Of Delphic-pulsing timelessness across millenial-epiphanic
Suspensions of marble-streaming, Pachelbel-dewed horizons;

The Meissen-crystalline pool of water lilies beyond fragile
Chimeras of time, creating its own coronal apex
Of Rembrandt-veined light transforming the sun and god
Into amaryllis-incandescent swallows of Promethean-amber
Light shaping Orangerie memories in garland-glowing, dove-
Whispering helixes of saffron-consecrating light and rosary-
Tendrilled, mosaic-auroral chimes of Giverny-permeating,
Bronze-gloaming mirrors.

# THE WIND IS A DIONYSIAN SHARING

The wind is a divine mind
Of featherless, motionless luminescence

The wind is a St. Anthony lament of the dead
A fragile-streaming solstice-prophesy of Siddhartha

The wind is a Dionysian sharing of time
In pristine voices of bronze-pressed asters
And saffron-sheltering, Botticelli-scented camellias

The wind is a transatlantic mirror of crocus-mazed light
A Primavera resonance of Aristotle
Contemplating the bust of Homer

The wind engraving indigo-vaulted paroxysms
Of Avalon-incandescent wisdom on crystal-
Auburn lithotints of time.

## In Swan-Gloaming Blossoms

A delphinium-blue afternoon sky saturates
The onyx-silver horizon in lily-adagio
Phoenix-wings of Borghese silences and amaryllis-jade
Helixes of Vedic-quantum silences,
Amber-silicon cataract-pulses of cypress-wombed hours
Congeal in cedar-veiling, saffron-acacia suspensions
Of ethereal-gray, sphinx-scented clouds,
Aureole-ivory breaths of light suffuse the sky
In swan-gloaming blossoms of diamond-orange,
    temple-dewed light.

# THE SOUL OF THE FOREST

When you walk between the two amber-majestic,
Dusk-ethereal pines at the Artemis-wreathed edge
Of the amaranth-celestial forest and tread softly,
Mellifluously on the golden-brown needles
Your soul enters forever the pristine-evolving domain
Of vernal-flaming vigils and you become forever
A part of the soul of the Ruisdael-burgeoning forest

Within the Thoth-sacred grove
A red and a white candle
On the primrose-permeating sides of a Chartres-
Breathing amaryllis-spire on a Tintern-fusing
Spectrum of silently receding mahogany-glass

Where the moon plays a cypress-vined fiddle
Of mellifluous-mazed light as the sun shapes
Emerald-scented pilasters of Nostell-leavening
Timelessness

Where yellow-teeming melodies of renascence-veined
Light perceive pink-rustling assonances of anemone-
Diastolic, apocalyptic-magenta dawn.

# THE VOICES OF THE CLOUDS

In the Murnau-red wind the voices of the Chillon-reflecting
Clouds scatter minaret-azure dreams of sunset-diffuse graves
Across orange-tympanum horizons in amethyst-pealing,
Norham-solitary tears of laurel-veined, lemon-diastolic light

The cathedral-transmuting voices of the Fontainebleau-
    ascending
Nepheliads sing nightingale-inviolable epiphanies of ancient-
Crystalline vastness where fiery-pastel asphodels bloom
In the saffron-opulent eyes of the palomar-isled divine
In crimson-lambent cascades of Isis-lyred resonances

In the narcissi-tremulous wind I hear the Aegean-pale reveries
Of twilight-vaned cloud-poppies splaying cosmic-diaphanous
Inundations of amaryllis-cinnabar stars across Utenwarf-
    timeless
Voices of white-ripening, turquoise-deepening spaces.

## An Infinity of Sensibility

There is an infinity of sensibility
In a gray-permeating, white-orisoned sky
Which the blue heavens can never offer

I am the gray-leavening spirit
Of the Aegean-vernal, oleander-rhythmed
Light suffusing galvanic-red horizons
With lichen-ochred veils of Pentelic-
Marble palms

Only the sepulchral-wise clouds
Know the nasturtia-whispering truth
About the world in amber-vaulting reveries
Of vermilion-canopied towers and autumn-
Prophetic, cross-refulgent dawns

Only the dove-brooding, rainbow-consuming
Clouds dissolve the maenad-raging, moon-
Cursed crags of mortality in Apollonian-onyx,
Willow-fermenting streams of Friedrich-altared,
Crepuscular-golden light.

# IN THE TEMPEST-DRIVEN HEART

In the Azay-tapering shadows of the jasmine-knolled
Linden-trees I see the Ionic-fusing silences of the past
Waiting for ruby-destined galaxies to nurture them
To alpine-bowered fronds of pale-conjuring delight

In the tempest-driven heart of the primrose-streaming
Pines I hear a melisma-wild shape rise to meet muse-
Weaving visions of the heliotrope-framing sky, amber-
Veined reveries of gazebo-solemn vows germinating
Lily-deepening pools of Wynyates-madrigal light

In the Paphos-tameless whirlwinds of the chameleon-
    preserving
Forest I see the dark-chanting shades of minerva-ancient
Sycamores listening to Florentine-mazed amplitudes
Of dithyrambic-glistening light yearning for nocturne-
Gladiolus wings of sphinx-resolving diasporas.

# THE KINETIC-AUTUMN WIND

At the dyke-fluttering edge of the ark-poised horizon
The Windsor-gloaming aureole-vortex is the final
Gaze of the agape-shattered divine in arborealis-
Pulsing, myrtle-congealing waves of aster-soaring
Light, Goldau-listening seagulls wandering in a tympanum-
Softening pastiche of phosphorescent-granite lulls
Miles from ocean havens Archimedean-veiled swallows
Floating across juniper-duned silences in the end
Only the kinetic-autumn wind conceives sea-fevered,
Hibiscus-shaping dreams of Atlantis-converging silences.

## GAZELLE-WHITE CYLINDERS

Gazelle-white cylinders of asphodel-pure light
Gather crystalline-eaved intuitions of calico-
Murmuring, dusk-voyaging equinoxes along the emerald-
Diminishing edge of the crescent-madrigal, acanthus-
Golden rainbow as the evening sea washes providence-
Swelling winds into Aegean-lost gardens of maroon-
Sepulchral light, Promethean-spired steps floating
Lavender-silken tendrils of muse-whispering
Calyx-webs in auburn-lyred silences of fugal-
Evergreen, perpetual-sage light.

# THE SNOW-SHOWER

The snow-shower is a pearl-misting waterfall
Of mercurial-shadowed incense lost from magenta-arked
Chalices of emerald-androgynous light by divine
Memories dispersing cypress-pergola omnipresence
across maroon-cusped thresholds

Corinthian-astered shapes of ancient-tabernacle silences
And gargantuan-mullioned silhouettes of Catskill-
Chancelled willow-cairns congealing time
In crystalline-jagged epitaphs of fate-tendrilled winds
pulsing myrmidon-tallow reflections

Of white-enameled whispers into pitch-apertured,
Dusk-arable abysses of shale-rarefied breaths
And astral-orange light where solstice dimensions
Of perpetual-sage souls transform moist-calyxed
Filigrees of time into millenial-pealing
redemptions of eternity.

# The Mist People

In a tetrahedral-mazed river of grey-knelled
Fog the mist people rise to watch the sky
Vanish in a purple-cymbal haze of mandrake-
Androgynous winds

Towns and villages masked and moved by crocus-
Alabaster splashes of sulphurous-circled light
Into another dimension of time
Where the mist people reign on auburn-marble,

Nemi-apocalyptic thrones of delta-winged clouds
As the silver-layering sea washes time away
Into a Balleroy-frescoed lagoon of hibiscus-
Jettied, calypso-leavening dreams;

The mist people shaping a new blue flower
Of Delphic-gloaming, saffron-pealing light
In the leviathan-veined, mobile-swirling atrium
Of the philomel-sacred, mimosa-reflecting glade

When diamond-pulsing eyes of almandine-shelled
Light conceive archipelago-crimson veils
Of Wallington-evolving, narcissus-fragile dusks.

## A HIDDEN LAKE

A hidden lake beyond Maggiore strands
Of sapphire-crenellated, marsh-trancing light
A lonely-jade spring of lunar-ranging tendrils
Of soft-eclipsing eyes and canal-domed,
    Luxor-greening tombs
A woodland stream of regina-lavender
Cotopaxi-palms floating autumn-clover bayous
Into the mimosa-gloaming heart of the sun
A pristine-rushing waterfall of Montmartre-anemones
In a mandarin-vaulting vase of marigold-
    stamened time
A delta-orange oracle of heron-sunset light
Weaving damask-ancient silences of crystalline-
    knelled, saffron-melisma winds.

## NOTHING BUT SEA AND SKY

Nothing but sea and sky
In a sirocco-endless dialogue of Sappho-surging rhythms
Splashing furtive-blue echoes of Aegean-silent wisdom
Across crimson-distending memories of auburn-weaving,
Allegro-persisting horizons,

Nothing but sea and sky
In crystalline-fusing trilogies of rolling-green mirrors
Sweeping amethyst-fated reflections of yellow-veined,
Pergamon-binding mountains in ancient-iridescent waves
Of silver-winding, Gautama-spanning oracles,

Gargantuan-androgynous breakers of mecca-quivering crests
Conch-seething cries of bone-shrill seagull-solitudes
Tantra-swirling crescents of madrigal-haunting swallowtails
Soaring across marlin-pandora lattices of Byzantium-
Witnessing, minerva-lavender silences.

# THE FLOWER OF ETERNITY

A lavender-cloistered haven on a cypress-ardent island
In the middle of a palm-breathing, russet-trembling
Windermere-reverie where the damask-inventing,
     ultramarine-
Iridescent flower of eternity assimilates flames
Of verbena-resined bloom, an embryo of palatine-
     rhododendron,
Orange-spindling light dispersing lunar-rippling seeds
Of Janus-stamened life, promontory-apsed veins of diamond-
Mullioned timelessness concentrated in dusk-heaving hearts
Of candelabra-enamelled stones conscious of Fauve-
Immutable inner harmonies instinctively listening
To the dynastic-tendrilled wind shaping the voice of eternity
In jade-ringed reflections of rainbow-preserving, aureole-
Murmuring silences, stones only touched by rhapsodic,
Curving breaths of a few immortal souls watching over
The saffron-restoring, muse-resplendent sublime.

# THE MORNING DEW IS A DANCE OF DIVINE WHISPERS

The morning dew is a dance of divine whispers
Shaping the first surf-tendrilled, Pleiades-surmising
Waves of Artemisian-lavender, gladiolus-soaring light
In miramar-venerating, cypress-floating reveries
Of dahlia-luminescent, mandala-pervading eyes

The morning dew is a purple-misting tarantella
Of mountain-swirling light shaping the auburn-
Crystalline sea in sundial-mahogany preludes
Of azalea-refulgent incantations in aquamarine-
Liminal nocturnes of Matisse-pink-discoursing
Horizon-mirrors

The morning dew is a red-globed oasis
Of salmon-androgynous, delta-winged silences
Conceiving sapphire-lambent, asphodel-pure synergies
Of Aurora-sophic, silken-altared omens and lilac-
Sparkling, Orangerie-sunset ballerinas.

## Of Auburn-Etching Lazarus

Ivy-trellised rhythms of saffron-furrowing light
Converge the divine-softening eye in cypress-fluent
Haloes of luminous-lavender topiary-lullabies
Brushing across amoebae-tinted capillaries of olive-
Sated time where a blue-marrowed wave of Aegean-lost
Sunlight marvels at a yellow-spectral sage of manna-
Chastening light; sun-channeling covenant-tremblings
Of auburn-etching Lazarus console emerald-sulphurous
Fritillaries of white-thatched time in autumnal-silver
Helixes of half-timbered, marionette-sketching dreams
And Salisbury-arching rainbow-metamorphoses.

# A Clock Rides Upon the Sea

A clock rides upon the sea in a sedan
    chair of astral-trembling light
A cloud seeds the sky in hermetic
    intimations of aquamarine violins
A mist of Aphrodite-silvering melancholy
    saves the amaryllis-plunging curves of the sunset
A thought of the divine congeals
    in an amphora of equinoctial light
A web of muse-whispering silences
    transforms time in mandolin-intuitive masks
    of crescent-apertured shadows
A piazza of synthetic-diagonal wafers
    pronounces the lunar-suspending order
    of the orphic-mazed harlequin
A line of diamond-margined music staffs
    agitates the sumptuousness of mortality
A détente of curvilinear-pink harpsichord-
    convergences and heart-vaulting tower-murals
    prophesies the purity of the blue-sacramental circle
A mountain of yellow-sailing light
    plays pristine-discordant chords of perpetual-
    sage harmonies across cypress-layered dreams
      of Castalian springs.

## The First Sounds of Spring

An aureole-mazed breath of light burgeoning softly
Suddenly among gray-torrential, sphinx-sceptered clouds,
A divine spark of onyx-white lucidity giving life,
Radiating iris-diastolic blossoms of fugal-trembling
Life across windmill-sharing memories and Breakers-
Luminescent reveries of evening horizons,
A camellia-marble breath of pure damask-prismed light
Pulsing the first moments of auburn-jonquil mandalas
In moist-jade tendrils of sea-fevered dreams,
Shaping the first sounds of spring in amber-gray willows
Of lunar-rippling, diamond-apocalyptic light and soft-
Languishing, cyclamen-solstice prayers of russet-
Spiring winds, floating Easter-stamened lilies
In amaryllis-empyrean estuaries of mandrake-germinating,
Arcadian-lavender sunrises.

## Of Glynde-Spacious Eternity

I listen to the dusk-pealing amaryllis-lambent silences
Of ancient-lacquered shadows meandering
Through jade-apsed clearings of Camelot-enthroned
Wilderness as the hourglass-congealing breeze
Radiates violet-weaving whispers in heliotrope-
Softened crannies of agaric-widening tombs

I am the white-cairned, lotus-astered perpetuity
Of stone-martyred silences suspending gray-stained
Dooms of Venus-thorned light in lavender-oracular
Cupolas of Delphic-crystalline, Eroica-unvanquished
Reveries;

I feel the cypress-consoling silences of the Barlach-
Reciting stones in my hands lichen-dreaming etudes
Growing into my hands nepenthe-pallid euphonies
Filling my hands with andante-coronal pulsations
Of onyx-inner, alcaic-saving wisdom

I feel the Rodin-elegiac stones sharing pantheon-
Moist whispers of Glynde-spacious eternity
With auburn-resined bands of mourning-dappled
Flesh shaping my hands in dusk-glistening
Intimations of crescent-apertured, gold-enflaming
Light.

## A MADONNA

A madonna among the soft-prismed apples slowly
Shaping rivulets of zinnia-exulting, acacia-
Consecrating timelessness along velvet-sirocco
Curtains of dream-furling, ivory-plumed light
As the saffron-gelatinous wind breathes dahlia-
Fetal shadows across Ephesian-gloaming hills of
Red-onyx palms, a face of obelisk-radiant depths
And evening-fermenting silences sealing Katmandu-
Lavender timelessness in crocus-culminating aureoles
Of Maya-lemon hibiscus-doves.

# A Damask-Scrolled Fugue

The evening is a damask-scrolled fugue of amber-
Terracotta light shaped by solstice souls in hermetic-
Stringing, Himalayan-magenta dissolutions of time
And sacred-liminal harmonies of amaryllis-eaved
   helicon-solitudes
Solstice souls rising from sphinx-willowed,
Wessex-stamened silences creating Aeolian-lavender,
Brahman-pealing triptychs of twilight sky in dahlia-
Fermenting, cypress-exulting helixes of grail-sceptered,
Magnolia-tiffany reveries
Solstice souls carving mandolin-crimson intimations
Of Mahakala-lotus eternity on porcelain-gray cloud-
Monoliths of Rhine-primordial, juniper-breathing
Energy as the adagio-spectral wind perpetuates
Horus-anemone exodus in apocalyptic-christened,
Kithara-apsed amplitudes and autumn-lacquered, silver-
Leaf aureoles of Turner-iridescent, golden-architraved light.

# In Mimosa-Yellow Incantations

As the mist clears I see apocalyptic-white angels
   playing the Chillon-auguring ritual of timelessness
   in Dogana-yellow globes of lily-breathing,
      astral-latticed light

As the mist clears I see twilight-amber
   temple-pallors falling upon the castle ruins
   engraved in myrrh-evening, azalea-diaphanous
      silences

As the mist clears I see the hyacinth-golden light
   emanating from the eye of the divine shaping
   sacred-alluvial tremors of eternity reunifying
      amethyst-sealing wisdoms of ancient-textured
      horizons with cypress-wandering islands

Of Jungfrau-suspending gladiolus-truths, when the mist
   clears I see marigold-seraphic butterflies dissolving
   time in mimosa-lavender incantations of diamond-ethereal,
      autumn-helixed light.

# THE SUNSET CLOUDS

The sunset clouds are soft-decaying, chamomile-
Straying angels of palomar-isled, Pissarro-eaved light
Magenta-pealing mournings of serpentine-angled,
Levitan-astered light amaryllis-pulsing, Dogana-
Sentient echoes of marsh-templed, lotus-harped light
Shaping the Amazon-undulating, Elbe-celebrating flame
Of gargantuan-persevering life in the space
Of a few lilac-chasmed, porcelain-helixed moments
Suspending time long enough for primordial-cinnabar
Castalian-souls to enter the Maggiore-veined,
Uffizi-valed prism of bronze-pealing eternity.

## OF SACRED-ANEMONE SILENCES

When the sea washes upon the shore
In the late afternoon it leaves traces
Of divine silences and saffron-exulting
Truths, traces of ancient religions and
Distant mythologies which the children
Pick up and cast away as broken,
Extraneous seashells on delta-wandering
Filigrees of Poseidon-whispering spray

When the sea floats upon the evening shore
Marble-auguring omens of other galaxies
And Gemini-soft pallors of eternity
The children think they look pretty
As pink-silken ribbons blowing carelessly,
     loosely in the breeze

When the sea washes its carmine-soaked
Tears upon the twilight shore the children
Laugh and play catch and try to capture
A fiddler crab nestled in the sand

When the sea washes its last swells
Of sunset-stained star-embryos upon
The candle-knelled shore only broken-
Prismed traces of sacred-anemone silences
And Atlantis-permeating aureoles linger
At the crimson-luminous, sulphurous-circled
Edge of eternity.

# Autumn

Autumn is a delicate symphony
Of soft-madrigal swallows and albumen-
Crimson nirvanas of jen-amber light

Autumn is a diastolic epiphany
Of amaryllis-chancelled space, a systolic
Mirror of gelatinous-emerald time

Autumn is the cyclically reciprocal
Revelation of Nature and God
In a fragile symbiosis of seraphic-
Ascending visions and indigo-angled prisms
Of fern-camellia hieroglyphs

Autumn is the gathering of yellow-marrowed,
Cinnabar-jade ambrosia by a Buddha-wandering figure
For the iris-glowing soliloquies and silver-
Polygonal folds of her poppy-arching winter-dreams

Autumn is a crystal-dewed transformation of time
Into embryonic, dynastic-sharing trinities
Of honeycomb-diaphanous, magi-eternal light

Autumn is an inner radiance of vale-horizoned,
Saffron-conceiving leaf-souls of cypress-marble purity
Shaping new dimensions of acropolis-shadowed,
Helicon-pinioned timelessness.

## ALONG THE AVALON-MISTING SHORE

Elysian-petaled seashells strewn along the Avalon-
Misting shore in moor-globed tides of laser-blue,
Alzinen-spinning thoughts, emerald-mimosa
Annunciations of Poseidon-radiant sunlight
Glistening along crimson-drenched thresholds
Of algae-languishing, soft-barnacled time,

Andromeda-amber silences floating crepe-myrtle
Mantra-swallows of pandora-philomel light
Across Flensburg-cloistered incantations
Of russet-orange dominions and maroon-havened
Prophesies of Vermeer-softened lucidity,

Auburn-concentric pulsations of Elbe-tinted sunsets
Streaming cerebral-jade poppies of calliope-
Aquamarine silences into cypress-expansive caverns
Of metropolitan-mercurial time.

## Bronze-Parabled Leaves

Ahimsa-stamened time drips from ginger-evolving
Leaves like almond-scented honey from autumn-
Sheaved, Nirvana-moist combs
Locust-molten blooms of Ghent-oleander light
Shaping the edge of time from sepia-chaliced
Tremors of the Tibetan-fugal evening wind
Bronze-parabled leaves searching for peregrine-
Jade souls, waiting to congeal as acacia-golden
Butterflies in the patient hands of the palomar-divine
Pale-willowed wings flying south in an orange-
Templed glaze of Shiva-pulsating mists
Gemini-aureole leaves spilling time into chalices
Of yellow-terracotta light, shaping eternity
In ancient-emerald mirrors of platinum-sheer obelisks.

# The Purification

Let the platinum-quivering waves ripple through
Your hands in crocus-ethereal surges of sunset-
Globed silences, let the carmine-maenad chimes
Of the snow-porcelain sea flow through the salmon-
Duned ventricles of your soul in miranda-languishing
Echoes of limestone-burgeoning time at the Gemini-
Lavender threshold of life, let the silver-moist light
Of the sea cleanse your mind in soft-diaphanous
Tonalities of Venetian-white nocturnes, let the ocean
Feel your abalone-enchanted love for the saffron-eternal
Truth of its mimosa-scarlet, magi-discoursing horizon.

## THE VOICE OF ETERNITY

The wind is the Rheinstein-immaculate voice of eternity
Casting dune-fountained visions of margrave-wandering
Souls onto sea-leavened canvases of Byzantine-tessera
Horizons as a solitary figure gathers helicon-pulsing
Sheaves of dusk-golden light in his cinnabar-glowing
Hands and in the Aegean-moist corners of his mind
Shaping them into nirvana-gloaming whispers
And albemarle-gesturing shadows of arborealis-chastening
    cloud-haloes
A daily absolution of chiaroscuro-rising, spire-
Reincarnating energy of the ancient-martyred,
Palladian-wise self,
A transformation of the cumulus-mazed self
Into sulphurous-violet, crimson-refining confessions
Of the Parthenon-twilight sun,
A renaissance of the diastolic-crystalline self
Into the first saffron-petaled intuitions and purple-
    sceptered breaths of the evening wind.

## Let the Autumn Fill Your Soul

Let the autumn fill your soul with Elysian-cosmic
Sadness with the hydrangea-fluted melancholy
Of piazza-apparitional evanescence as impetuous, red
Leaves glisten through your hands for only the soul
Embalmed in Dogana-wise sadness can prophesy
His own imminent, unvanquished eternity
In Zoroastrian silences of magenta-crystalline light
Let the sea fill your crocus-raptured soul
With astral-mazed chasms of sapphire-tameless,
Giorgione-melodious light
The Belton-twilight wind shapes the darkness
In odyssey-silver chimes of daemon-ethereal loveliness
As the sea seals time in Florentine-pale eyes
Of lapis lazuli-wandering sculptures of amber-
Vaulting, hyacinth-echoing light.

# OF HELIOTROPE-MIMOSA DAWN

I walk out of marble-dewed, willow-meticulous silences
Of the evening-crenellated abbey into crocus-
Sceptered lights of pink-chrysanthemum suns
And Lethe-gendered, dusk-unvanquished resonances
Of ancient-limestone Indian-summers
As Hyperion weaves Lorelei-softening traces
Of gypsy-dreaming time into polymer-stamened
Haloes of auburn-telestar castles
As Sappho scatters plum-crested waves
Of alabaster-edged memories into Hibernian-
Coved epiphanies of kithara-beige light
I walk among the sepulchral-latticed breaths
Of bronze-whispering light listening
To the crimson-sage swallows whispering
Alluvial-ochred spells of heliotrope-mimosa,
     orange-acanthus dawn.

# AN AMETHYST-GLISTENING PETAL

The gray-whispering, amber-veined clouds have a profound
Wisdom said the northern wind far beyond that of the
    pallid-blue heavens
A wisdom of sibyl-converging stones preserving heliotrope-
Mazed visions of damask-silvering eternity

The majestic-blue, topaz-radiant clouds have a supreme
Wisdom said the southern wind far beyond that of the
    alabaster-gray endlessness
A wisdom of sea-inventing, turquoise-architraved
Echoes of cedar-permeating eternity

Only the amaranth-crystalline light of the Pythian-listening,
Carnation-weaving evening knows the truth as it shapes
Sunset-tympani in Nolde-gloaming helixes of candelabra-
    magenta melodies;

The clouds smiled upon me in their marble-effulgent,
Pastel-galactic magnanimity lifting my soul
Into their hibiscus-expanding, lapis lazuli-conceiving
Mists where I saw the mandrake-confessing, iris-brooding
Gardens of eternity illuminating the Harlaxton-towering
Dome of heaven, in the emerald-singing, chrysanthemum-
Glowing silences I heard asphodel-pulsing reveries
Of lily-germinating, Turner-iridescent light
I became an amethyst-glistening petal of the Hesperus-
Eloquent cloud-heart floating on Isis-cascading
Intuitions of Aegean-discovering, Atlantis-divining light.

# THE SOUL OF THE LAKE

On a moist-purple, sun-shrining July morning
He understood the soul of the lake
As he gazed into the dark green-pervading silences
He understood in his innermost soul
The Chopin-pristine language of the windswept ripples
As he sat in melancholy loneliness along the reed-misting
Banks his soul became one with the willow-sentient
Waves with the ribbon-flowing geese
With the purple-languid rushes with the amaranth-
Leavening soul of the divine pool
Crystalline-jade ripples perpetuating the lotus-
Radiant permanence of their own incarnate
Profundity, he spoke to the waves softly
And the waves spoke back caressingly
Sharing their genesis-persistent wisdom of immortality
With a nature-prophet bound to the deluge-
Nurtured beauty of their perpetual-listening silences
And then the breeze ceased and the lake
Became as clear as jasmine-diaphanous harmony-glass
In the depth of the waters he saw
In a minerva-pallid mirror the soul of the lake
Shaping timeless rhythms of Gemini-green light
In a Beethoven-liminal epiphany of asphodel-blossoming,
Emerald-lyred beauty he saw the lily-vaned
Silences of his own soul.

# THE TWILIGHT-APOCALYPTIC REVERIE

The twilight-apocalyptic reverie is the purest
Crystalline-chancelled light of the evening sun
Amber-epiphanic annunciations of golden-veined,
Delphic-sated light suspend time in marble-
Perpetual haloes of Sesshu-solstice spirits
Wandering across sequoia-peristyled, cypress-vaulting
Thresholds, cobalt-glowing, cinnabar-rising
Effusions of orange-evolving, Parthenon-helixed light
Healing the wounds of mortality
Transforming Gautama-musing souls into arborealis-
    lingering
Echoes of Harlaxton-dawning light
Shaping the Easter-dewed hieroglyph of the horizon-
Leavening sun in amaranth-lavender memories of eternity
As iris-stamened prophesies of porcelain-acanthus,
Maroon-prismed light open forever the bronze-pealing
Gates of paradise.

# OF DIVINE-GLOAMING WISDOM
## AND EDEN-EXALTING SPACES

# THE WINGS OF SWANS

In the wind I hear the gray-astered, fugal-converging silences
Of the divine floating against silicon-curving pillars
Of eternity swirling around agate-misting pilasters
Of ancient-templed shores, in the late-afternoon wind
I hear soft-alabaster voices speaking of millennial-white,
Contiguous dimensions of time where mortality is only
A prelude to reincarnation,
In the wind I hear empyrean-softened, ethereal-groved voices,
Blue-adamanthine reflections of juniper-cresting voices
Calling from cerulean-swathed mountain-amulets,
The late-afternoon wind breathes anemone-gelatinous
Omniscience through magenta-emerald gates
Of Brahman-pealing paradise,
In the wind I hear the wings of swans bearing souls
To Nirvana-rising thresholds of saffron-onyx light
In Atlantis-duned silences I hear fragile-violet
Kelp-winds from the Mycenaean wilderness beneath the waves
And astral-yellow cypress-winds from the end of the world
Shaping the immanent timelessness of the damask-weaving,
Nocturne-spinning self.

# THE SOURCE OF IMMORTAL TIME

Wandering through Nepal-blue flowers of chrysalis-
Delft dreams I see the embryo of immortal time
Pulsing vermilion-porcelain veils of dahlia-tensile
Light across the sable-altared edge
Of the acropolis-sunset sea

A magnetic-jade shaft of crimson-arborealis
Angles in a marsh-haunting, madrigal-laminating
Pool of salmon-androgynous, sulfurous-circled panes
Deepening into Promethean-scarred abysses and ancient-
Towering, Pleiades-sealing ruins of the castle of Egmond

Wandering through blue-sceptered tulips
Of dune-layered, myrtle-calyx fields
I see the onyx-veiled source of immortal time—
A helicon-orange bouquet of dusk-fragile, amaryllis-
Leavening silences and marigold-chastening,
Amstel-spacious light-murmurs—
In an Atlantis-crescent radiance of sylvan-parabled
Waterfalls and Sargasso-stained winds.

## ECHOES OF ETERNITY

Along the hieratic-willow, moss-satyred pier
I see limestone-moist echoes of eternity
Floating across ancient-lintelled, Artemis-jade horizons
In mantra-rustling elegies of lily-trembling breezes,
In the pumice-architraved vortex
Of dactyl-inventing, crystal-eclipsing waves
I see the amber-prismed radiance
Of marble-Parnassus chimes scattering
Delphic-veined rivulets of dithyrambic time
Across marigold-embering sands of lunar-sheathed light,
Along the edge of asphodel-symphonic silences
I hear seagull-crimson, azure-perfecting murmurs
Of the Pythian-white clouds of eternity.

## A Sculpture of Orange-Chasmed Leaves

A sculpture of orange-chasmed, Eucharist-eloquent leaves
And soft-marlin, columbine-triadic infinity rises
Through acanthus-vaulting traces of crescent-morning mists,
A white-veiled sculpture of ancient-lambent
Truth and tympanum-fugal silences scatters
Wild-anemone murmurs of Picasso-kithara light
Across Sistine-auguring fields and Flemish-ringed pools
Of lichen-glazed, cathedral-shaping solitudes,
The light of the marble-expanding sculpture
Infusing the light of the sun
With onyx-maroon pulses of divine-alcaic radiance,
The light of the silver-scrolled sculpture
Dissolving time in a Doric-floating mirror
Of crystalline-cypress, sublime-amber light.

# THRESHOLD MOMENTS

It is only at threshold moments
That we are truly alive to the genesis-
Lavender beauty of the crystalline-
Architraved wind and to the divinity
Of the saffron-helixed light of our souls,

It is only at threshold moments
That we breathe Nirvana-almandine omens
Of alcaic-tessera light and transform
Our souls into perpetual-amber twilight-
Cadences of Sylt-vestal, wind-dreaming eternity;

The poem is a luminous-solstice epiphany
Of the transcendent and transforming self
In Apollonian synergies of Monet-burgeoning light
At the lemon-exulting, Lhasa-rippling threshold
Of eternity,

The poem is a Michelangelo-gloaming purification
Of ephemeral time, a transformation of mortality
In sacred-liminal, timeless-golden silences
Where the lyrically resonant spirit never changes
And the karma-soft, reincarnating soul never dies
The poem is a Limoges-pristine resurrection of the dusk-
Ripening self in purple-oracular, diamond-lintelled
Pools of eternity.

# Four Sacred Forms

A castle of magenta-dewed, peacock-creched silences
And adamanthine-shearing, Parsifal-ranging soliloquies
Transforming vicissitudes of time
Into orange-cascading, pearl-fluting megaliths
Of Arnhem-resined, amphibrach-soaring light;

A castle of poinsettia-germinating, bronze-sublime
Harmonies of apocalyptic-crimson winds
Redeems white-shadowed caravans and jade-apsed crevices
Of spectral-vanishing carbuncle-energy in Gemini-
Sacred prophesies of Atman-thalassic, silver-equinoctial light;

A castle beyond scythe-laminated dreams of time
Beyond sable-totemic murmurings of mortality
A perpetual-amber eclipse of time in a majestic-
Martyred, magi-pristine cove of the Thames,
The Rhine, the Hudson, and the Ganges
A crystalline-leavened simultaneity of eternity
In poppy-wandering, dusk-sated thresholds
    of cypress-helixed light.

# A DAHLIA-GLOBED OASIS

A dahlia-globed oasis of saffron-mandarin light
Along an ethereal-Dardanelle cove
Of the angel-pulsing, paladin-dusted river
A velvet-golden palace of a hundred majestic-
Amber spires of cinnabar-obelia light
Shaping Mediterranean whirlpools of lavender-
Sated sky into isis-cascading hieroglyphs
Of fern-winged light, agate-kithara tears
Of afternoon-delta winds transforming
Time-furling waves into onyx-pale reveries
Of Delphic oracles and Stonehenge-auburn
Helixes of pomegranate-lily hibiscus-dreams,
A palace of a thousand crimson-molten, lambent-
Orange crystal-windows holding the soft-pink
Light of eternity in anemone-spinning,
Damask-aureole mirrors, acropolis-spanning,
Isthmus-silver walls of Pindar-jettied light
Ascending Windsor-enameled crescent-mountains
Of slate-chaliced time, purple-jonquil sails
Of mural-fermata, sphinx-veined light fading
In astral-delphinium arbors of sage-misting,
Catskill-apteryx haloes.

## Of Dusk-Gloaming Mirrors

The Minerva-gentian light is the Elysian-pale radiance
Within the lotus-germinating soul beyond meridian-
External suns of myriad galaxies as intrinsically
Powerful as the Saltram-exalting light of the auburn-
Breathing chandelier illuminating the heliotrope-sheaved
Heart of Delphic-golden reflections only in a marble-
Pilastered, lily-converging vortex of dusk-gloaming mirrors
Is the light onyx-pure and Apollonian-soft only in a spacious-
Crenellated epiphany of sphinx-magenta auras and
    ogival-diapason
Chimes does the saffron-leavening light heal the wounds
Of mortality in lavender-asphodel, Harlaxton-winding
    silences.

## An Ethereal-Sage Castle

An ethereal-sage castle appears near the Orangerie-
Enclosed lake when the amber-helixed, Theocritean-
Softening twilight pours across its Belvedere-cascading
Walls and disappears in the azalea-fountained light
Of the lapis lazuli tears of diving spirits dreaming
Of Palladian bridges I saw it once in my youth
When the Sistine-cairned elms reached Parham-giant
Shadows along the edge of the azure-swelling waters
When onyx-stained breezes whispered eglantine-streaming
Harmonies in maze-fermenting lullabies when madrigal-purple
Butterflies played upon saffron-gloaming rhythms
Of Zoroastrian-seminal light there is a Gothic-liminal,
Moss-reflecting castle dividing transience from the asphodel-
Veined shadows of immortality sheltering the lemon-scrolled,
Daemon-sealing auras of eternity from ephemeral-gilded,
Sable-ewered words in the presence of the diamond-paned,
Opalescent-globed castle the questing soul reshapes itself
In dawn-perfecting calligraphies of phoenix-soaring,
Tyntesfield-effusive, emerald-calyxed light.

## OF DIVINE-GLOAMING WISDOM

There is a savannah-lambent day when
The red-solstice pulse of eternity
Chastens lavender-entombed tears and mortal-
Laminating thoughts along Eurydice-marble
Matrices of odyssey-satyred winds
When the inner glow of saffron-Elysian light
Heals all the animate and inanimate life
And makes all things papyrus-whole, Maya-vaulting
Visions of divine-gloaming wisdom
When the sea and sky are an Apollonian-onyx
Unity of blue-albumen, gray-webbed light
A vermilion-profound reverie of oasis-
Alveolar intuitions encompassing amaryllis-pink,
Thrush-gracing cloud-helixes
Communing with Orpheus-noble beings
From a jasmine-remote, Lindau-binding curve
Of the yellow-polygonal horizon
A dynastic-anemone meiosis of Nepenthe-hyaline,
Zodiac-consecrating memory transforming pisces-sunset,
Morven-pendulous megaliths to hermetic-lavender
Murmurs of dove-winding eternity.

# A Timeless Moment

A timeless moment when you see
The beginning and the end of time
When you see endless orchid-augurs
And eternal-spindling filaments of space
When you understand sapphire-swelling murmurs
Of the evening wind
When you know what it means for a crocus-masked leaf
Of the soft-gnarled sycamore to blow in Ruisdael-embering
    breezes
When you understand light-flowing rhythms
Of damask-rolling robin-speech

A timeless moment when Sanskrit prophesies
Transforming passionate-palomar thresholds
Transmuting marigold-striated harp-whispers
Shape Dionysian helixes into columbine
Echoes of Apollonian infinities,

A timeless moment when the last rays
Of the sun possess all the wisdom of the world,
When all mortal wisdom
Is framed by a canticle of light
When all mortal wisdom
Rests on the mist-tapered ends of a great white pine
Alone in a corner of the alluvial, windless forest.

# A Stone-Breathing Manor House

There is a stone-breathing manor house at the edge
Of town on a cypress-helixed meadow leading
To the Ionic-phosphorous center of the earth
Dark-crimson tunnels pulsating inner rhythms
Of diamond-mantled light across juniper-
Marrowed thresholds of coral-sheaved eternities
A hieroglyph-vaulting Shangri-La
On lily-rolling hills of soft-forgotten time
Majestic gardens of orchid-hibiscus dreams
Beyond sable-thrusting vicissitudes of transience
A soul-shaping Shangri-La of divine-fugitive silences
And amber-veined epiphanies of jasmine-amaryllis light
A Florentine-chancelled prelude of harp-musing truths
Inevitably flowing to other worlds of dusk-frescoed
Trinities and orange-prophetic, Turner-iridescent immortality
A marble-grottoed paradise of magi-murmuring winds
And maroon-syncopated sunset-vigils.

# THROUGH MARBLE-MISTING EONS

A room where the saffron-helixed light of eternity
Fuses with the cypress-amber light of immortality
In a perpetual-sage, lotus-harped suspension of time,
A palomar-frescoed dimension of the timeless self
Sealed in dusk-crystalline tremors of Delphic-sated grace
And astral-dewed configurations of green-purifying infinity,
A Rembrandt-veined solstice soul safe forever from
The calico-jettied gestures and pitch-draped dreams
Of mortality pressed helplessly against adamanthine-
Veined, diamond-apteryx walls,
A solstice soul losing itself in maroon-prismed reincarnations
Of chrysalis-anemone voices radiating lavender-onyx
    cathedral-
Silences through moss-crenellated centuries and Appassionata-
Swelling, marble-misting eons of time.

# THE FIGURES IN THE PAINTINGS

There is a time of day
When all the figures in the paintings
Emerge in the spaciousness of the room
When they sit on the divan or along
The mahogany table and talk freely
As if nothing had happened
As if their willow-murmuring essences
Were as perpetual as the cyclicality of nature
When they appear from gilded frames
And chiaroscuro eternities, from Gothic-liminal
Reveries and azure-unvanquished spaces
They never change endowed by the arabesque-golden,
Acanthus-lintelled enclosure with the Blickling-
Luminescent aura of marble-germinating eternity
They never fear the vicissitudes which ravage
The flux of the world and time
Shaping the tremors of the sea along the calyx-
Mazed dream of the horizon conceiving dune-scented
Meadows in diastolic epiphanies of yellow-exalting
Light in the ethereal-primrose, amphora-echoing
Gleam of Meissen-amber silences the figures fulfill
A twilight paradise in mandrake-eloquent shadows
Where lavender-resplendent asphodels and Delphic-
Pealing, lily-gloaming reveries never fade.

## OF ATLANTIS-SHAPING SOULS

In the monumental shadow of the White Mountains
There is an Eden-conscious, helicon-serene valley
Of lily-gloaming solitudes and onyx-lavender snowdrops
Where centuries ago a divine figure wandering
Across celestial domes of pale-acropolis dawns
Inadvertently dropped a vial of alabaster-fugal silences,
An Aeolian-charted vale of hawthorne-trellised
Timelessness where Atlantis-shaping souls live forever
In the emerald-lyred, minerva-gentian beauty of nature
And in centripetal synergies of cypress-regenerating
Radiances, a crystal-vapored, ochre-sensitive valley
Of ethereal-marigold, pink-tessera light
Where time is a ravine-furrowed memory
Of Giza-shattered vows, a soft-forgotten echo
Of Parthenon-sated augurs,
A valley where the light of inner beauty
Is as infinite as the light of the sun.

# The Pristine Tapestry

Meissen vases shaped in silken-ochre
Pools of ancient-anemone pagodas,
Porcelain-lambent calyx-trinities lingering
On fragile-carillons Ming-thresholds
Of twilight-crocus moors, emerald-
Floating chalices of Luxor-pale light
Lost in sunken synergies of sand-corniced,
Rainbow-delta incantations,
Dynastic-frescoed pyramid-dews spread dawn-
Crystalline passions of amber-prophetic sunsets
And rosary-seething, toccata-membraned cantos
Across shrill-evergreen omens of Cytherean-
Syncopated centuries, immortal-filigree
Silences scattering the chiliastic-sceptered
Darkness in Shadwell-hermetic vigils
Of lilac-knotted, amaryllis-reflecting eternity.

## Shaping Ancient Cosmogonies

I listen to the sylvan-canyoned silence of the rain
Shaping ancient cosmogonies of Venus-spinning light
Bone-tenuous echoes of eternity linger in marble-sheathed
Spaces crossing between gale-shimmering lines of arc-fated
     time,

Primeval pearl-filaments of Toledo-ethereal light
Burgeoning across vesper-palmed fields
Of Barlach-furled darkness, sable-staccato
Fountains of jasmine-crescent light surging
Through Phoenician-tempest veils of samovar-
Arching chambers, nomadic beads of auburn-molten
Light sealing porcelain pauses of time
In cormorant-subtle souls of palomar-isled,
     soft-chasmed winds,

The coral-scented loneliness of stone angels penetrates
Dusk-laminating aureoles of a divine mind
I see the plume-eeled, cinnabar-pyramid silences
Of eternity in hermetic-purple asphodels
Of amber-purifying, kelp-gyrating light.

## Of Ivory-Tympanum Silences

There is a cobalt-gloaming piece of pristine-
Veiled eternity in the Hudson-spiral patch
Of forest wilderness outside my window
A chime of calypso-elixir eternity in the goldenrod-
Maned blossoms perpetuating crystalline-
Amaryllis mists of marlin-Gibraltar timelessness
Where God lingers on pastel-blue wind-helixes
Of bronze-mourning, poppy-wandering light
Where elves carve gold-mullioned
Blooms of alabaster-apostrophic light
On Catskill-ancient texts of soft-forgotten voices
Where almond-rippling butterflies and straying souls
Of autumn deer perfect liminal truths
Of ivory-tympanum silences and
The sacred longevity of bluebell-stained time.

## As Emerald-Amorphous Breezes Vanish

Only a convolvulus-astered ruin traced by Ionic-
Fading furrows where once the abbot's house stood
Now moss-distending stone burgeons in peach-dappled,
Melisma-fraying lights as emerald-amorphous breezes
Vanish into Elizabethan-soft peals and Gothic-ravined
Echoes of Penshurst-lost dominions, Langenburg-fusing
Souls languishing at the sable-cairned edge of eternity
As moly-elliptical abysses cluster in sibyl-divergent perfection
A jade-misting reminder of the past, a marble-pallid
Reflection that everything animate, even Tiber-meandering
Stones, passes away in the Foscari-willowed corridors
Of dune-rusting mortality—only fragile memories
Of Einsiedeln elegance linger in the omega-shrined visions
Of the Corinthian-vaulting spirit of the Valle Crucis-
Sceptered ruin for time never separates kindred souls
And their Promethean-blossoming, diastolic-orange dreams.

## OF MAGENTA-VERNAL HIEROGLYPHS

An oaken-gabled line of pilaster-terraced white
Where the oleander-misting sea meets the dahlia-
Curving shore in a lilac-molding ecstasy of triadic-
Urned deluges a rosewood-tapering pastiche of madrigal-
Shearing fountains filters adamanthine-glowing sunrises
Through the portico-yellow ruins of a Tivoli-ancient
Graveyard Iliad-pale names whitewashed by candelabra-
Splintering silences saving the dead from the draconian
Vicissitudes of hourglass-sated rituals a crystal-trimmed
Sacristy of magenta-vernal hieroglyphs preserves the bronze-
Winding castle of the soul a Veronese-refulgent fresco
Of fleur-de-lys-concealing seeds of Polyhymnia delight
Shapes oriel-crossing masks of Caen-sutured heavens
As campanile-turquoise stained-glass pink-lunettes
Blow gently across sacred-opalescent, Ionic-looming glades.

## Through the Heart of Time

Damask-Gregorian suns of apteryx-green light
Calibrate soft-webbed dawns of orange-jasmine
    solstice-altars
In aster-congealing benedictions of arborealis-petaled
    echoes
In sublime agate-hexagonals of mist-privileged
    acanthus-dreams,
Wandering through soft-globed gyrations
And lithium-engraved draughts of the heart of time,
Confessing Phrygian strands of willow-arched resurrections
Across amulet-grey apertures of kinetic-lemon
Fragrances, praising anemone-breeding,
Sulphur-exiled, phoenix-veiling eyes
Of acropolis-veined, ibis-spiring night-winds.

## CORAL-ADAGIO HELIXES

Coral-adagio helixes of blue-sceptered, Vishnu-canticled
Dreams conceal archipelago-runed fantasies of lunar-
Softened light in Iliad-furtive ascensions
Of marble-globed parabola-echoes,

When the sea moves from the frosted beach
It takes an ambrosia-carved sigh of sphinx-murmuring,
Crescent-slivered silences of evening suns shattered
On sirocco-caned dirges of brandy-pearl, gaunt-pristine shores

When the sea moves from the hawthorne-dewed beach
It saturates moon-plasma Hebrides-soliloquies
Of latent children's laughter and onyx-bridled anemones
With oleander synergies of calico-toned gloom

When the sea moves from the twilight shore
It takes eternity along to a palomar-isled dream
Of amber-soaring epitaphs of willow-vaned light
And leviathan-blue dissolutions of carillons-fevered dawns.

## In the Briny-Spectral Deep

In the briny-spectral deep of alluvial-grey anemone-silences
There is a cavern where time began
Where the first rainbow-surging pulses of time
Flowed from indigo-onyx prisms of poseidon-
Tentacled, auburn-linteled coral-dreams,
A Delphic-languishing lagoon of arborealis wisdom-amoebae
Where time is a motionless, opal-sheathed wind
Of sapphire-helixed jonquils of light
Where time is a soft-flowing whisper of jade-
Sutured eyes of myrrh-pristine epiphytes
Where time is an Ovid-terraced memory
Of shrill-tympanum counterpanes and archipelago scansions
Of crimson-marble sunset-myths
Only eternity lingers in amber-turquoise meioses
Of ochre-wombed light and pale-winnowing annunciations
Of hydrangea-streaming calliope-haloes,
Perpetuating zodiac resonances of Mediterranean-astral time.

## Of Rosary-Incarnate Light

White plasmas of coniferous Aeneid-light
  Pinpoints of painless amœbæ-dreams
    Escaping time in phoenix-scattering vortices
      Of chrysalis-anemone psalms, peripheries

Of Venetian-green destiny span elegiac delta-rushing
  Stamen-loams of translucent-magenta rainbows
    And poinsettia-flickering reliquaries as pink-orange
      Gyrations of moon-widening light suspend saffron-adagio

Memories of eternity in palladium-glistening, silver-
  Sinewed helixes of Sistine-astered tendrils, fern-cascading
    Mirabelles of marigold-virginal eloquence and damask-
      Primordial dawn-cadences fusing Michelangelo-gloaming

Prophesies of rosary-incarnate light in Geneva-leavening
  Amplitudes of fugal-yellow accompaniments, radiating
    Lichen-solstice dusks in lapis lazuli-expanding, Passacaglia-
      Breathing mirrors of amaranth-crystalline, Elysian-converging
      Light

# An Orphic Heart

Deserted silences lie about the eaves
In philomel memories of ancestral quartets
Only time is forgotten when autumn
Prayers purify the lucidity of beauty,

Three cylinders of wax-glowing light descending
From an intuitive, porcelain pause
Of elegiac-sweeping sky onto hidden covenants
Of acropolis-still corners and motionless, onyx-veiled
    pallors,

A rimless word flowing into infinity
An orphic heart converging in chrysalis-vermilion myths
Of ambivalent annunciations, returning
To a lilac-tinted hourglass.

# OF THE POPPY-BREATHING CHANDELIER

In the heart of the pomegranate-sceptered mirror
The lavender-germinating soul can see vulcanic-sage
Reflections of the poppy-breathing chandelier
In the Florentine-astered depths of the dusk-gloaming
Mirror the saffron-iridescent, Monet-crystalline soul
Can see the birth of the laurel-architraved chandelier
In sibylline-dewed atrophies of emerald-cascading light
In the Jungfrau-spherical, mistral-gesturing chasm
The marigold-listening chandelier becomes an Aeolian-vaned
Lily of madrigal-turquoise feelings spreading its Janus-
Diapason wings through grail-oracular corridors
Of the universe as the sea becomes an amber-vaulting dream
Of Eden-liminal, Meissen-labyrinthine light.

## SALISBURY-MYRRH INCANDESCENCES

I listen to Salisbury-myrrh incandescences of wind
And vernal architraves of snow-lavender light
Shape hemlock-gestating time into Fountains-solitary
Reveries of anemone-cascading, cross-latticed eternity,

I listen to orchid-misting aureoles of ancient-Chaldean
Seas and lambent-carving oracles of sphinx-surpassing
Pines redeem time on marigold-jade thresholds of Schleswig-
Silver, limestone-arbored silences.

I see time congealing in a palomar-weir
Of rhododendron-stucco, apricot-tenoned light
As the wind-clover glistens talisman-white
Along the Andromeda-nape of the hyacinth-myrtle moon;

I see time in a cinnabar-quartz carafe
Of pink-setting suns and marble-olive fountain-spells
Waiting for butterfly-doves of orange-molten light
To rise in megalith-arching, Prague-blue memories
Of stained-glass, sun-dusted silences.

# THE VIRGIN OF THE ROCKS

Amaryllis-pink sands contemplate moist-pearl
Capricorns of Rhadamanthus madrigals,
The virgin of the rocks suspending jonquil-jade lulls
Of time in saffron-adagio haloes of hydrangea-blue light
Shaping Stygian-architraved vagaries of time in Auvers-
Helixed, sirocco-softening whispers of seraphic-crystalline,
Chartres-acanthus repose as a solitary figure sits along
The damask-embering canal waiting for vernal-diaspora,
Sans Souci-luminous truths floating cirrus-white, pastoral-
Eglantine breaths of empyrean-diastolic sky onto camellia-
Silken petals of ethereal, pristine humanity.

# A SILENT-SOLSTICE FIGURE

A silent-solstice figure gathering sophia-andante
Filaments of purple-seraphic light and pristine-
Amphora vowels of pearl-cruciform, reliquary-misting
Overtures from the crescent-aboriginal moon
To give to the divine-veiling, Aeolian-white presence
In the middle of an alpine-cathedral valley of Fulda-
Red poppies and grail-lavender lily-reveries,
A silent-solstice figure shaping juniper-
Kinetic transubstantiations of moist-acanthus time
In hibiscus-cascading statuette-haloes of phoenix-
Marsh silences and frankincense-nightingale truths.

## Of Elysian-Prophetic Eternity

The dance of the stars is the beginning of eternity
Stars reshaping time in alabaster-fluting mournings
Of orange-diapason, autumn-musing light stars redeeming
Space in green-diffusing sails of emerald-syncopating light
Stars carving vermilion-lingering cloud-nocturnes
And pearl-gazing, horizon-articulating windmill-solitudes
On amber-presuming, perpetual-mirabelle sunsets
The light of the dance is the only lodestar
Of zephyr-raising dreams and tempest-eclipsing moons
The figures of the dance become the Venus-binding
Pilasters of Elysian-prophetic eternity
The figures of the dance are the seraphim-radiating
Seasons of violet-acanthus helicon-melodies
And the piazza-irreversible laws of Kedleston-mazed destiny.

# THROUGH THE MOON GATE

The one who passes through the moon gate
In a gardenia-fluent perfection of fuchsia-striated light
Becomes a Shen Chou-pervading spirit of the stone-trellised,
Amethyst-hermetic grove where ancient-mandarin mysteries
Of perpetual-alabaster silences shape gloxinia-burgeoning
Tremors of emerald-discoursing diasporas in miranda-veiled
Glyphs of camellia-scented eternity where the soul
Who cherishes the rainbow-ascending fragrance of acanthus-
Congealing, yellow-musing, lotus-carving graces becomes
A Giverny-primordial essence of the Chatsworth-enchanted
    truth
Of the sublime-vernal soul of the celestial-prophetic,
Tiara-glistening orchid where the soul who walks across
The ruby-crenellated, Gemini-seamed bridge enters forever
Elysian-whispering, Minerva-spiring auras of dusk-architraved,
Pyramid-confessing immortality listening to cypress-jade,
Atlantis-radiant murmurings of acropolis-singing waterfalls
Listening to the vermilion-profound incantations of willow-
Cultivating, mandrake-dewed sages.

# A VILLAGE BEYOND TIME

A village beyond silently massive
Auburn-duned thresholds of mist-tapering time
Beyond indigo-apertured nightmares
Of alabaster-sunken horizons suddenly appears
As a saffron-jade shower of crystalline-autumn sunlight
Penetrates a russet-chimed Gothic spire—
A cyclamen-lingering epiphany of perpetual crocus-veined
    twilight,

A village of eternal autumns
Rises from cypress-grey cumulus-swells and pomegranate-
Haloed fields of orchid-stained dreams
Only a few days of chrysalis-dewed existence
In mortal time
A village disappearing softly in its own eternity
An architectonic flaw of moist-seamed time
A forgotten, forever-languishing truth
Of amaryllis-chancelled, prism-architraved time
A village shaping its immortality
In Ruisdael dreams of luminous-embering
Angelus-suns.

# In An Elysian-Petaled Cove

In an Elysian-petaled cove at the purple-sabbath edge
Of the titanic-foaming falls there is a Chamonix-hallowed
    village
Of Flensburg-lucid permanences and butterfly-mimosa
Cupolas where time, as night, passes away in the Sistine-
Chastening radiance of philomel-auroral prophesies

A symphonic-astral oasis of Poseidon-nurtured
Silences and mercurial-jade ecstasies
Of russet-trembling, dew-glazed light
Beyond rose-engraving serpentine-mountains
And sirocco-cresting leviathan-plains

A gladiolus-converging sacristy of sapphire-
Etching dreams and Andes-aureole visions
Nestled in poppy-cloistered, turquoise-mantra
Pools of Corot-effulgent, Aeolian-lyred
 Twilight

Where the inviolable-glowing shadows of evening
Cascade through peacock-discerning, narcissus-
Conceiving layers of Versailles-rippling,
Gargantuan-auburn mirrors into marble-architraved
Dawns of crimson-hermetic synchronies
And chrysanthemum-radiating, virgin-pealing solitudes.

## THE SPIRIT OF THE MANSE

In the amethyst-streaming, Wynyates-enclosing mist
Of jonquil-maned, almandine-equinoctial silences
I see the spirit of the manse rise above the myriad-
Astering roofs and pink-variegated turrets becoming
A sacred space of jasmine-rolling hills and amaranth-
Dewed lawns where maple, oak, and pine blossom daily
In pristine-exalting fountains of orange-diapason,
Camellia-architraved light I am the silver-leafed,
Attingham-wise spirit of the manse shaping gardenia-veined
    chalices
Of crimson-languid melancholy into flamingo-shadowed trees
Of Gemini-sceptered light I am the emerald-conjuring
Spirit of amber-timeless valences suffusing the gate
Of ancient-heraldic signs with my Venetian-exiled,
Hibiscus-latticed dreams reshaping mimosa-lonely hearts in
    damask-
Haloed crocuses of wild-empyrean innocence

Along the hyacinth-breathing edge of the Palatine-misting
River is a grail-conceiving castle where the heliotrope-
Exalting silence of the Delphic-golden light redeems
The longevity of time where maroon-asphodel silences
Recreate the Schönbrunn-perpetual pallor of willow-vaned
    love.

# A CHANDELIER OF MAROON-CONTEMPLATING LIGHT

He crossed the garden of Botticelli-astral smiles
Towards the almandine-breathing light in
   andromeda-lithesome
Visions of Goya-petaled night shaping the sky in Fasanerie-
Laminating isles of adamanthine-sceptered liberty
Upon a Baroque-gesturing urn of Chagall-musing fame
Where ormolu-gentle willows turn beyond the emerald-
Germinating horizon in Chambord-gusting panoplies
Of topiary lullabies and dew-shining flames;

A trumeau-revealing chandelier of maroon-contemplating
Light in the lily-effulgent mirror of Hesperus-cadenced,
Marigold-synthetic dreams twelve Delphic-inviolable eyes
Of onyx-madrigal, Pythian-white light luring me
Into the Florentine-mazed aura of the orphic-fulfilling,
Jade-scrolled frame opening the sacred-pilastered, crystalline-
Acanthus fold of eternity dissolving a diastolic-meandering
Soul in Blickling-lambent effusions of golden-mullioned
   gleams
Transforming Ruisdael-gentian intimations of the divine
In auburn-gloaming aureoles of odyssey-helixed epiphanies
In wisteria-oracular pulsations of amaranth-cascading,
Eroica-soaring light.

## IN THE GREAT CHAMBER

In the Great Chamber
You don't have to worry about headstones,
Graveyards, or eulogies you can spread
Your soul out on the turquoise-paned marble
As if you were entering a Chenonceaux-crystalline frieze
In the Great Chamber
You can congeal time in amber-angled vapors
Of onyx-mullioned light where the sea is a sibyl-
Wounded reverie of amaranth-templed silences
Shaping autumn-winged intuitions of eternity
On diaspora-helixed solitudes of sphinx-resolving vases
In the Great Chamber
You don't have to drink ambrosia-tinted elixirs
Or scream about the absolute frailty of a god
Who condones perpetuities of suffering
You don't have to believe in wooden crucifixes
Or clay figurines in pastel-veneer beads
Or cranberry-glass words you can seal the Aeolian-
Gossamer tendrils of your saffron-diapason soul
In tarantella-white constellations of asphodel-pulsing,
Lily-chanting twilight.

# THE GHOST AT KENILWORTH

In the gray-spindling evening the ghost at Kenilworth
Walks through the tiara-plumed, oleander-corniced portal
And the Gemini-astered priory-gate into the jade-apsed
Mists of the heliotrope-conceiving, Byzantine-furrowed
Cemetery where every grave awaits his gentle-mitred,
Hieratic-gleaming caresses where every grave knows
That he will bathe magenta-liminal helixes in the yellow-
Amaranth light of his nepenthe-linden soul
Where every spirit, recently buried or centuries old,
Feels the semblance of eternity in the cumulus-graceful
Magnanimity of his dynastic-martyred presence
The ghost at Kenilworth shares damask-pinioned globes
Of Aeolian-effusive light with diastolic-amber souls
Rising from wine-stamened, cypress-germinating pallors.

# A Castle of White-Hummingbird Silences

A castle of white-hummingbird, asphodel-confessing silences
And purple-witnessing, pellucid-green mirrors permeates
The final edge of the iris-weaving, Sylt-vestal horizon
Where ancient-trembling cobwebs sparkle
In dusk-sated angles of omniscient darkness
Where dew-centered epodes of butterfly-amber light
Distill higher laws of Dunham Massey-vaulting eternity
A castle of silver-purifying, chrysalis-lavender silences
Surrounded by an Aeolian-hexagonal moat of pristine-
Leavening timelessness shelters empyrean-radiant, moor-
Astral breaths of solstice souls perfecting the Eden-
Ascending, lichen-globed visions and emerald-flowing
Hieroglyphs of their divinity.

## In Emerald-Veiled Panoplies

A Mansart-effulgent castle of tabernacle-gray, ivy-wreathed
Silences emerges where Zarathustra-liminal lives rest
Like mosaic-pristine leaves on frost-tipped, pointillist-
Glistening marsh-staves, a pergola-seething, baroque-ringing
Castle where Tudor-inflecting, parapet-listening souls live
Forever in Lido-breathless stillnesses, a Jacobean-panelled,
Grail-enchanting castle where the nabi-intimate, dawn-
   eglantine
Promises of talisman-projecting, amaranth-prophetic tapestries
Are fulfilled in emerald-veiled, diastolic-yearning panoplies
Of hermetic-altared, Matisse-crystalline light conceiving
An auburn-vaulting singing-tree in the Marburg-sacred
Courtyard beyond the ruby-ephemeral smiles shaping saffron-
Architraved melodies of Montacute-streaming timelessness
In velvet-spinning murmurs of twilight-extending, asphodel-
Blossoming eyes.

# An Orpheus-Reigning Oasis

A dance of twelve amaryllis-merivale premonitions
  around an emerald-gazing dusk of Arcadian silences
A dance of twelve Rheims-littoral skull-veils
  around a mahogany-smiling, diamond-laminating plateau
  of pink-adamanthine clouds
A dance of twelve honey-breathing, rainbow-conceiving
  elves around a harpsichord-oval grove of orange-mazed,
  arborealis-tympani melodies
A dance of twelve alabaster-jade leaves
  around an ancient-Phidian, silmarillion-valed oak
A dance of twelve shaman-graceful martyrs
  around a tremulous-stone, spiral-inventing aperture
  of amphora-gusting paradise
A dance of twelve okisa-heightening seagulls
  around a moist-carving memory of dune-victorious,
  Salome-transposing nocturnes
A dance of twelve saffron-juniper, Klee-dreaming rays
  of flamingo-gloaming, Tintoretto-distending light
  around an Orpheus-reigning oasis of sphinx-hermetic,
  marigold-dawning timelessness
I am the Chartres-conceiving soul of the crepuscular-
  lambent, Golgotha-orange light of astral-lintelled,
  crimson-onyx timelessness healing apocalypse-scented
    soliloquies of Elysian-dewed hearts in Goldau-
    immaculate, andante-chrysalis euphonies of mandrake-
  flaming, Bernini-soaring light.

# THE FIRST CYCLE OF MORTALITY

In the molten-spherical odyssey of calico-angled
Mortality I shape twelve lives of onyx-lavender,
Marble-gesturing vastness refining the thirteenth
Ephemeral dimension as the perennially immortal self
In the first cycle I reshape orison-tempest
Tablets of wax-forgotten, Moses-ravined noons
In Arcadian-sunset megaliths of amaranth-diastolic, Stygian-
    crystalline light
I transform dusk-sated, Sistine-exulting
Murals of iris-gyrating, ivy-trellised reflections
In jade-perfecting vales of Eden-liminal, Aeolian-swelling
    mirrors
I reveal sophia-marigold silences of anemone-
Purifying light along the Wessex-prismed threshold
Of a lambent-rising empyrean-lake sheltering
Ancient-lingering, mist-stringing souls
I carve millennial-silicon, rune-congealing contours
Of the divine in amaryllis-hexagonal eaves of diamond-
Lintelled winds and kithara-chancelled tremors of silver-
Compassionate, Seebüll-cerulean souls redeeming
The nirvana-saffron timelessness of the inner self.

## In a Timeless Vale

An asphodel-paned, lavender-cullised house
Of bronze-germinating light in a timeless vale
Unseen by mortal eyes where time is only
An echo in the pristine-suffusing radiance
Of Easter-pink clouds, where time is
Only a fleeting breath on the soft-eternal
Innocence of Vermeer-immaculate light,
Where time is only a refraction of coronal-
Turquoise space in seagull-empyrean murmurs
Of the grain-latticed, Vedic-arborealis wind,
A Saltram-luminous, cathedral-sheaved house
Where I live forever in hermetic-autumn aureoles
Of helicon-conceiving pine-sceptered light
Sealing saffron-exulting memories of orchid-
Veiling, Gethsemane-moist dreams in Uffizi-shaping
Frescoes of golden-astered, sacred-liminal light.

# A SACRED-LIMINAL WELL

I distill marigold-prophetic, apocalyptic-astral mirrors
Of amethyst-diastolic, psalm-evolving light
From amaryllis-unicorn veils of sable-ewered darkness,
I fold triadic-coiled vestiges of Tintern-engraving
Time in calliope-pealing, symphonic-astral blooms
Of chrysalis-autumn moons as the zodiac-
Permeating wind carves Glastonbury-moist emblems
Of Mycenaean-kylix light on a cobalt-globed baptistery
Hovering over Thrasemine-eaved pools of ancient-
Votive, iris-misting silences—a sacred-liminal well
Healing the wounds of mortality in wisteria-
Trellised, orange-diapason ripples of zinnia-exulting,
Linderhof-crystalline light.

## The Caretaker of Time's Garden

Along the edge of the abyss
He climbed into the sable-gesturing, jade-
Angled mists of the granite-cased, white-
Rustling waterfall where the castle of time
Lingers in ancient-rubied shadows of primordial-
Duned eternity, among fir-sceptered boughs
Of cypress-almondine light he wove moss-amber
Filigrees of syrinx-galed time into a Rhine-dusk
Constellation of Eleusinian-legato petals,
Among autumn-tendering, tempest-softened calligraphies
Of Tudor-pealing, gentian-pulsing light he revived
Lavender-gypsum, acacia-voyaging voices of jasmine-
Crystalline, albatross-veined cairns and glacial-white,
Lichen-arching loch-souls in spacious-crenellated,
Cosmic-marble epiphanies of jonquil-diffusing,
Nirvana-sealing wisdom, he became the silent-honored
Caretaker of time's garden with its own astral-deepening,
Rainbow-enclosing, grail-ascending, apocalypse-
Spanning beauty, in consecrating himself to shape
The garden in lily-cascading, poppy-germinating frescoes
Of celestial-Florentine, amaranth-perfecting light
He endowed himself with the sage-sublime aura of eternity
The hierophant-soft, ichor-burgeoning inner light
Of eternity radiating across hermetic harmonies
Of aster-mazed, thrush-murmuring horizons
Of damask-lavender, Aeolian-dewed light.

# A Castle by the Sea

There is a candelabra-gloaming castle by the twilight sea
Where time is only an apse-scented tremor of Melpomene-
Eglantine light where Sistine-azure harp-murmurs shape
Sibylline-vaulting reflections of turquoise-coronal space
In Giverny-effulgent waves of saffron-adamanthine light
Weaving Eden-liminal, poppy-breathing dreams
Along the Amsterdam-tempest shore,
There is a Tudor-luminescent castle by the evening sea
Where one never grows old watching the Dogana-pink frailty
Of grey-cullised time behind porcelain-silver panes
Of salmon-sheaved, Ruisdael-glowing light listening
To astral-labyrinthine omens of the ancient-prophetic wind
Fill the sky with Fountains-tremulous voices of rosette-
Ivory melancholy and apocalypse-ringed, fern-creased
Mirabelles of pearl-shadowed, Persephone-lambent echoes,
A Neuschwanstein-spacious castle of onyx-anemone, pine-
    sceptered
Solitudes where silent-solstice, heliotrope-revealing souls
Carve dove-abiding margins of lavender-architraved genesis
On coronal-magenta rainbows of diamond-immaculate cloud-
Synergies sealing purple-asphodel silences of sapphire-
Incarnating lilies in Elysian-lambent, almandine-hermetic
Epiphanies of Apollonian-sage, sunflower-exalting light.

# AFTERWORD

I have never met Hugo Walter in person. We live on separate coasts, swim, so to speak, in separate schools. I don't know the color of his eyes or what kind of car he drives or if he even drives a car. We correspond a bit and speak on the phone, but our letters are brief and to the point, and our conversations are cordial and businesslike. I don't know the man Hugo Walter at all. I know only one thing about his personal life: he writes poetry.

On the other hand, I know the poet Hugo Walter well. I have had the pleasure of publishing five previous collections of his work (this omnibus gathering of selected poems makes six). And I will say this: in the twenty years that I have been publishing poetry, by poets of all stripes (iamb-fettered neoformalists to free-verse liberationists, classicists and romantics, moralists, feminists, doggerelists, catalysts, you name it), I have never come across another poet like the recognizable and yet unclassifiable Hugo Walter.

I once made the statement that Hugo Walter has reinvented the color wheel of the English language. What does this mean, exactly? If you've read the book in your hands, you know. If you've skipped to the back before reading the poems, I won't tell you what it means.

One gets the feeling that Hugo Walter sees life not through a microscope or a telescope, but through a kaleidoscope. He is a poet for whom impressionism is carried to the extreme: the impressions are not created by images. Rather, the images are created by impressions, the clash of juxtaposition. The technique may not be easily explained, but one thing is certain: it is original, it is unique to one poet, and that poet is Hugo Walter.

Walter's poems do indeed stand alone among poetry. Typical of his poems (though not exclusive to Walter himself) are the vibrant splashes of color, the driving meters, and the whirlpool of lush images. Even more striking are Walter's references to a shared, pan-national human culture that mixes Greeks with Orientals, the Renaissance with the Old Testament, and the art of Egypt with the paintings of Impressionism. But what is truly ground-breaking is Walter's highly developed word-play, a creative association of concepts that, by its very audacity, differentiates itself not only by quantity but in quality: Walter has invented a new style of poetry all his own. This is poetry that knows its own vocabulary, works in its own grammar, and has its own idea of syntax. In fact, it is not too much to say that Walter has invented a new poetic language. The purpose of this new language is to explore new frontiers of understanding: with his trademark style of hyphenating odd couples of beauty, Walter combines sensual visual images with concepts and interpolates references to antiquity from all ages and all human cultures, putting layer upon layer of thought and feeling, juxtaposing nature with art, music with base nouns.

Certainly if there is any message to the poems of Hugo Walter, the message must be found with you, the reader. Whatever you glean from these coined words, you can't help but be impressed by their impressionism, can't help reeling in response to this unusual poet's inventive use of linguistic skyrockets.

—J. M. DANIEL